GW00707497

OF LIFE AND LOVE

OF LIFE AND LOVE

Eight Moral Tales

Freddy Fynn

Matador
5 Weir Road
Kibworth Beauchamp
Leicester LE8 0LQ, UK
Tel: (+44) 116 279 2299
Fax: (+44) 116 279 2277
Email: books@troubador.co.uk
Web: www.troubador.co.uk/matador

ISBN 978 1848765 238

British Library Cataloguing in Publication Data.
A catalogue record for this book is available from the British Library.

Typeset in 11pt Aldine BT Roman 401 by Troubador Publishing Ltd, Leicester, UK

Matador is an imprint of Troubador Publishing Ltd

Printed in Great Britain by the MPG Books Group, Bodmin and King's Lynn

For late Elizabeth and late Kofi Snr.

CONTENTS

To find the meaning of life is to have a reason to live.

A KING'S LULLABY

The quiet night exposed the chirping of the crickets. For large toads, it was a time for celebration. It had rained in the afternoon and at the side of the road, little ponds had formed in the potholes. All the people in the village had retired to bed early that night, as the park in front of the palace had been soaked. Every window was open to allow the cool, fresh breeze from the tropical rain forest to lift the hot air released by the muddy walls.

He always came out in the night when it rained. Even though his kingdom was shrouded in darkness, his mental picture of the territory of Obraland (literally 'life land'), was so vivid that he could still see the small African village before him. His humble countenance belied his strength, but he could not resist a smile of pride. Each time he walked on his balcony, he would hear the village women as they talked about his wisdom and prowess. The women would shout their praise aloud, knowing full well that he could hear them.

His bravery in the fight for Obraland against the people of Mempe Ade Pa (literally 'dislike for good things') resonated as folklore at village gatherings. For the men, his identity was 'the king of justice and impartiality'. In times of disagreement, they sought his fair judgement for a perfect resolution.

King Solos (the nickname given to him by the people as they

always compared him to King Solomon), the wise king of Obraland, breathed deeply and pushed down his custom-made Adinkra shirt, allowing the air to circulate around his hairy chest. He yawned, stretched and tapped lightly on the wall. "Enough air, my lungs are full and besides I am already tired. I need to get some rest," he said.

He opened his door and went to his stool room. He sat on the lowest chair to feel how his subjects felt when they came before him. As he sat there, he felt the intensity his presence commanded in the people. "Is it enough? What legacy will I leave for my people?" he asked himself. He needed to deliver a message that would change the community throughout every generation. He smiled as his wise heart whispered to him. "Wonderful, wonderful," he said. Presently he rose and went to sleep.

During his reign, he had defied the old tradition and married only one wife. He had filled the palace with maidservants who attended him. Almost all the maids were children of the under-privileged; his way of ensuring that every one of his subjects was supported.

In the village, there lived three sisters named Abortre (Patience), Botaye (Purpose) and Shebre (Destiny). To carry out what his heart had whispered to him the other night, he called for Patience to come and stay with him. He insisted that she be the only maid who could get close to him personally. When the king was asked to resolve conflicts, he would have Patience sit by his right-hand side.

One day, Atta and Attong engaged in a serious fight over the division of their late father's properties. The whole town had gathered in their house, in order to seize the knife and sticks they held to each other's throats, ready to end their respective lives. The village folk immediately marched them to King Solos' palace and placed the two men before him. He sat there for almost ten minutes. "Bring me two bowls of sand," he ordered. All the people gazed in surprise, wondering what sand had to do with inheritance. He turned to his left and right, and demanded, "and bring me two boxes of needles." He emptied each box of needles into the two separate bowls of sand. "Pick them all out, one by one," he asked the brothers.

They began as the people watched. The first one rose up after just five minutes when he realised he could not pick them so easily. "I can't, I will not. What is this?" he shouted at the king. The chief executioner drew his sword at him for shouting at the king but the king motioned to him to put the sword down. The second brother painstakingly picked up all the needles in his bowl and raised it to the king, saying, "Long live my king, I am done."

The king smiled and stood up. "Gentleman," he told the first man, "I have every right to give all the properties to your brother. He deserves it. However, you managed to pick some, so I will give you part of the inheritance based on the amount of needles you have." The people began clapping in awe as they left the palace.

One fateful day, the king had a terrible illness. He called for Patience and told her, "Go to your parents and the community now, but call your sister Purpose for me. She will come and stay with me from now on."

Purpose stayed with the king throughout his illness and oh, what a happy man he was. Since Purpose came to the palace, the king would arranged for the whole community to gather every Wednesday night so he could tell them stories of life. Each time he told a story, he would leave them with questions and implore them to find the answers.

On the first night, with Purpose by his side, he addressed them. "There was a successful woman who supplied her entire town with most of their market's produce. She had a reputation in her business and realised that many of the town's men admired her beauty and fantasised about her.

"One day she stopped selling and began entertaining these men. She would go to their local beer parlour where they habitually gathered and 'entertain' them. It did not matter to her what kind of man enjoyed her company, only that he had money. She gained notoriety in this area and soon was the talk of the town.

"The men loved her services and she loved the attention. That is until one evening, when the men had gathered as usual, she had walked proudly into their centre and began dancing and suddenly the thrills and claps abruptly stopped. The men all started hiding their faces as they left the bar. What had they realised? What did she realise? I leave that to your conscience."

On another night, the whole village gathered once again. This time they all had mixed feelings and curious faces. They all wondered what was going to come next. The king emerged from his room with Purpose at his right-hand side.

He sat down and began. "A man walked into a bar to find the people within crying. He was curious to find out why, so he enquired and they told him the sad event that had happened. The man stood there for some time and then headed towards the owner. "Give me as many local beers as possible," he asked.

"The owner was stunned, but had to oblige. The man went to the centre of the crowd and started drinking the beer. Initially, the people were confused and did not understand. He kept on drinking. Then suddenly, the crowd became impressed because none of them had seen a man who could drink so much of the local beer and still sit there fit and conscious. For each glass, he would raise it towards the crowd as they cheered him on. Soon the crying bar had turned into a cheering bar. Everyone was happy, clapping and cheering as he kept on drinking. He left in a stupor, waving to them as he did so.

"Why did he do that? What did they get from it? Once again, I will leave that to your conscience." The villagers left more puzzled than the previous time.

Then came another Wednesday. This time, everyone in the village, even the old men who could not walk and were carried, came to the palace. The king came out from his room with Purpose.

He sat down and began his riddle. "A priest stood behind a pulpit. He glanced at the people and saw that they all had a dull expression on their faces. They seemed distracted in life. He started preaching on his favourite theme of hope and endurance. He spoke with such flair and convincing spirit. Then, he realised that the people sitting on the pews were now nodding and raising their hands in the air, absorbing the powerful message of hope. He could see he was changing lives and they could sense their lives being changed. He finished, waved at them and left.

"How did he feel? What did they feel? Once again, I leave that to your conscience but this time, I bid you all farewell."

That night, the king's sickness worsened: he was about to die. He called Purpose and said to her, "Go back to your family and the community. Ask Destiny to come to the palace and stay with me."

At the time of death, all his noblemen gathered around him as they had done to his predecessors. The first king, King Akate, confessed just before he died that he had misappropriated the royal funds, namely gold, for his personal gain.

The next king, King Abumba, confessed to killing a poor farmer so he could marry his faithful and devoted wife.

The penultimate king, King Kinpo II, confessed to using brutality on his subjects by imprisoning anyone who opposed his questionable judgements.

The kinsmen waited desperately for King Solo's confession. He glanced at the curious faces, coughed and finally began to speak. The silence in the room was so intense you could hear a pin drop.

"One's destiny is unknown as we do not know tomorrow. For me, I have realised that the desire of my soul goes beyond my achievements tomorrow. But the satisfaction of my soul today will last for eternity. I now rest with my fathers."

"Be the first person besides my noblemen to be at my grave," he said to Destiny. Then he died.

The noblemen shook their heads in confusion, as they fought to hold back their grief. They took his body to the ancestry chamber, performed the necessary farewells, and they buried him.

Adenda enstooled as a new king, it was customary for him to give a speech before the whole community. He wanted some of his father's wisdom, so he searched King solos' bedroom for inspiration. Underneath the pillow, Adenda found a piece of paper. It was King Solos' memoir.

It read, "Life is a journey - so I found out! But, how far and where to? Throughout life we must face many challenges and the best partner I can have is Patience. In all the hustle and bustle of life, what do I seek to achieve? What is my purpose in life? If I can discover my purpose in life, I will always be prepared to embrace my destiny. Is life just to eat, drink and make merry? It depends on my judgement! I had Purpose by my side to the end because I have fulfilled my purpose. I had Destiny by my side in my last hours of life because I realised that after patiently fulfilling my purpose, I was ready to embrace my destiny.

"However, in my patience, I still prevail because I know I have a purpose in life. I held on to my purpose in life because there is a destination in every journey. Why should I persist in taking life's journey if I have no destination? I might not know where I am and where I am going, but if I know how and what it takes, I am not far from my destination. I was patient in life, fulfilled my purpose and held my destiny in my hands. Farewell."

On the day of the speech, Adenda stood before the anxious crowd and addressed them. "The message I give you here today is for both myself and the whole community. I can only guide you with wisdom and devotion, but we each choose the paths in life we trail. However, if we get stuck on our paths and need a helping hand, let us try and always remember the king's lovely maids. We should be patient in life, fulfil our purpose and our destiny is in our hands."

The wonder of love is a secret unknown to man.

A DEEPER LOVE

At that moment, the whole atmosphere was dense, still and devoid of even the faintest sound. It seemed like nature had just stopped to witness one of the greatest beauties she had ever produced since the beginning of time. All you could hear was the sound of their breath. Both of them froze in confusion as they looked deeply into each other's eyes. Oh, how could James love her that much? What did she do right? If only he knew? As Lucille turned away to leave, tears rolled down the smooth contours of her face. Her mind drifted into the past.

The family's activities had begun unusually as all their relatives had come to celebrate Lucille's fifteenth birthday. She had wished for lots of things, but what more could she wish for when she was surrounded by the love and support of all her family? At the table, she could hear Grandma's faint voice telling her to make a wish before she blew out the candles. She leaned forward and wished, "I wish I will never grow old, so I can remain pure, innocent and without a care in the world." The flame felt the intensity of the storm from her 'blow'. Grandma took to the stage, as everyone followed, skilfully moving their waists and indulging in assorted food. Grandma fell down with a loud thud, breathless and motionless. Edward, her father, called for an ambulance. In that moment, the efficiency and effectiveness of the ambulance service deserved reckoning.

Grandpa looked up and saw Lucille crying profusely. He leaned forward and held her in his arms.

"Lucille, why don't you go home and the rest of the family will stay here with Grandma," said Grandpa. "It's not good to see this on your birthday, you know." Everyone nodded to show their concurrence.

Edward immediately rose to his feet and offered to take her home to keep her company. Oh, how he had shown her love as she grew up. She quickly ran into his arms as they left the hospital. Just as they were about to exit the main gate, she heard the loud cry of her mother. She instantly knew that the worst had happened. She turned to run back, but Edward assured her, "No, don't worry honey; I'm sure your mother is just scared for Grandma. Remember, Grandma always pulls through whenever she experiences such episodes," he said. Nothing sounded so soothing than hearing the assurance of the man she had grown to love and trust.

Tired and shocked from the days activities, she slid onto the bed and slept, although not deeply. On the precipice of slumber she heard angry voices in the far distance.

"Come on. Give me the combination to the vault. I swear if you don't, I'm gonna have to shoot you."

Another voice begged for mercy. "Please, don't do that, I can't. I just got the position and something like this happening…"

"Shut up, shut up. Just give me the codes."

She felt the arms of a hairy man lifting her skirt. She woke up and leapt with all the strength she could muster, but no, he was too strong for her. He turned, walked away without looking at her and said, "Don't ever come out." She could not believe what had just happened. Anger boiled within her as she reflected on where her father always put his shot gun. Then she heard the sound of a gun as her father screamed. Making sure they were gone, she came running out of her room to find her father lying in a pool of blood. Grandma was dead. Of that she was sure. What is going to happen to the family now, losing two members in one night? She knew what her mother was going to do. "I cannot live a day without him," her mother had said to her one night. The thought of what her mother was likely to do was too scary for Lucille. She would not be around to witness it.

She looked at the clock. It was nearly midnight. She quickly packed her backpack and fled through the window. The journey of no return! She began to quiver as she walked down the lonely dark road.

After about twenty minutes, she sensed the dazzling light of a truck lashing her back. A middle-aged man with broad shoulders and an innocent smile opened the front door. "Get in sweetheart; it's too late to be walking alone." She jumped onto the front seat, still wondering where she was really going. "So, where are you off to?" he asked.

She went blank for a moment then murmured, "I'm not sure. I just need to get out of here." For a moment, the previously unthreatening smile turned menacing. He stopped by the lonely road and pounced on her like a lion devouring its prey. He threw her out of the trailer and sped off. "What kind of world is this? I never knew such a brutish world existed until these past few hours. Why did they not kill me together with Dad? I would have been better off dead." She kept on repeating these thoughts. Battered, and mentally sullied, she limped slowly for half a mile.

She saw trails of lights ahead. As she arrived by the quiet town, she could feel her stomach clench. "Maybe, I could meet some kind strangers here," she said to herself.

A young man in drape jeans and a faded T-shirt sat by a fire pit, roasting some indeterminate meat.

"Hello sir, can I please have some? I am starving."

He laughed boyishly and handed her the piece in his hand. "Thank you, sir." He watched her as she gnawed the piece of meat with such ferocity. "Water?" he offered. He could tell she was choking.

Inside the house, he offered her a towel and soap so she could wash herself. She sat on the bed, bemused; wondering what could possibly come next. The boy came into the room and motioned to her. It was clear he expected something for his kindness.

"Please, sir, I have no money," she said.

He shrugged and tilted his eyes towards her skirt.

Early the next morning, she took off on her journey to the unknown. She had realised, that there is no such thing as a free lunch, well not with the men she'd met so far. The only way to survive these men was to play them at their own game. She found out that, even with that lifestyle, the challenges were beyond her strength. Tall, curly golden blonde-haired, and armed with a smile that made men quiver at her feet, it still wasn't enough, as the mature "workers" bullied her for her customers. She realised that she had to grow up as fast as she could. Walking the streets by night, a never ending and insatiable desire consumed her. She was a predator in the night. She could beat *these* men at any game they played. At least she had a small rented apartment and could eat anything she wanted, she mused.

Now armed with a depth of knowledge about the profession, she would blackmail any man that ever tried to outsmart her. She was good at that game.

As she sat in the back seat of the immaculate car, she realised that the man didn't say a lot. *Hmmm… a man of few words but a lot of action.* She smiled. "So, what's your price? I can negotiate any price," she said. The man kept driving silently. She got uncomfortable and started nagging at the man. "Okay, pay me now. I need my money." The man turned, perplexed.

"Excuse me, lady, I am not interested. I just wanted to help you get to the other side," he said.

Furious, she attacked the humble, innocent man. The man said softly, "Lady, if you had asked me for money for something, I would have gladly given you enough, but if it was in return for 'this'," he gestured at her body "then, I am sorry, I cannot give you anything." She exited the car, slamming the door behind her. "You will surely pay for this."

It was 1:00 am when the phone rang. He hesitantly walked to the phone as he grieved his lost sleep. "Hello. Listen to me, account number 000142572423, two point five," said the voice on the phone. He went numb instantly as he tried not to attract his wife's attention. "Who is this and what do you want?" he asked.

"I only want the point five and you can keep the two. If you know what's good for you, just go and put the money at the location I tell you. I told you you would surely pay." He dropped the phone. How did she find out? He became suspicious of his wife. "But I am convinced she doesn't know anything about this," he murmured. The following day, he went straight to a shopping mall and dropped the five hundred thousand dollars the caller had demanded. "It's all over," he sighed.

The following week, he could not believe it when he found his wife reading the morning news. "LOCAL CHURCH TREASURER POCKETS TWO POINT FIVE MILLION OF

CHURCH'S MONEY". What? But? What a heartless woman. His marriage ended about a month after the scandal.

Lucille, content with what she had done, sat on her sofa. At last, she was paying them back. They deserved it. She laughed hysterically.

"I am in control now. Nobody messes with me and gets away with it..."

She had just finished one of her usual long showers, but this time she could tell there was something wrong. She felt numb and could not move her body. Her temperature began rising. Within seconds, her whole body seemed to have ceased to respond to stimuli. She wished she could call a friend but she had no good friends she could call on. How she wished she had invested that money. She could have at least afforded to settle the hospital bill. "That's it! I guess I had my time," she said. Lying on the bed, she could hear her father's voice resonate, "You are loved, you were born out of love and you live in love." He would always tell her every night before she went to sleep. She had a wish, but this time, she whispered, "I wish a bird would come from afar and whisk me out of this depravity and suffering." She reached for a box of aspirin in the dusty cupboard and gulped more than the required dosage.

As the sun radiated with a reflection through the room, it shone upon a new 'woman'. She woke up in surprise. "I am alive. I am alive." She jumped from the bed and went straight to the bathroom.

"This is the new me. I can feel it. 'This' life is not my life. It's time to be who I really am."

She could sense her psyche yearning for a new discovery. She had to go back to being a 'kid' again. Will it be possible? She had seen and experienced too much to be a kid again.

She remembered when she would cling to her Barbie doll, pretending to be its mother. She loved the innocence and beauty of being a kid.

She walked down the alley, talking and chatting to the kids as she helped them find the best toys. She had finally made the right choice; that is, to work at the toyshop. At least, she could see and experience pure and true love from these 'little' angels who would not hurt a fly. She jumped and yelled in joy as a boy drove his car right through her legs. She believed that she was good with kids. She would reminiscence all night on how she was reliving her youthful life through the kids she met every day. The store manager would watch her unique display of attention and support for the kids.

"What an amazing woman. She is definitely a gift," he would say. Colleagues appreciated her so much because of her openness in life. "I am built for life," she would sometimes tease. If she could turn back the clock, she would start here.

"Come on, James. Get away from her." The angry mother shouted at her son. She walked furiously towards Lucille and pulled her son from her arms. "What are you doing with my son? You prostitute!" she cursed. Everyone at the store gasped in dismay. The look on her face exposed her guilt. "Why did my past come back to haunt me? Why not the good old childhood memories?" she asked herself.

Along the road, disorientated, she walked slowly, totally lost in her thoughts. Although she was thinking deeply, her mind was completely blank. She did not know what to think anymore.

"Hello, hello lady." She looked up and saw a man broadly smiling. "Madam, can you please direct me to 30 Grosvenor

Avenue? I have an important meeting there," said the man.

Composing herself, she pointed to the left and right in a vague description. "I am not sure I'll remember all that. Would you please, that is if you don't mind, get in the car and take me there?" he asked.

She sat in the car very quietly.

"Are you always quiet like that?" he enquired. "You look troubled. Is there anything wrong? Maybe I could do something to help." For the first time, she turned and glanced at the man.

"Oh, no sir, I am fine. I will be fine. Just..."

"No, no." he interrupted. "Don't get me wrong. I mean I just want to help you. I can tell you have a hard time trusting people. To start with, I will postpone my meeting for tomorrow and we can go to my house so I can get you some food. I am a good cook, I promise."

Why is he insisting we go to his house? Why not a restaurant or somewhere? They are all the same, she thought to herself.

"What an immaculate house! Everything is in its right place - no doubt the work of the woman of the house," she teased, nervously. *At least I will feel safer with his wife around.*

He happily hummed to the tune on the radio as he skilfully turned the steak in the pan. He was a master of cookery, she could rightly tell. Or maybe her senses were appreciating the odour too much because she was so hungry. He watched tenderly as she ate, it was as if she had been starving for days. "Here," he pushed another full plate of food towards her.

"Thank you, sir."

"No, don't, it's my pleasure," he said.

After she had washed down, he led her to a big room.

"You can sleep here. I will be across the corridor. Just shout if you need anything," he said. She stared at him agape. "*He will be back, I am sure.*"

She lay on the bed, restless, waiting for 'the usual' to happen. After about three hours, she knocked at his door.

"Come in. How can I help you?" he asked.

"I was wondering, I don't have any money to pay you for your kindness so if, you know, you want to, you can…"

"Stop that. Why would you? No, no." He placed her hand in his and caressed it.

"Thank you," she said.

"Don't mention it. The only payment I want is to see you happy. And besides, I would not do anything to ruin our sincere friendship."

On the floor of the room, she spread herself and began to sob intensely. She could not hide it anymore. *Who is this man? God, where was this man hiding all this while?* She sobbed as she fell asleep.

At dawn, she woke up before he did. She went to the kitchen and prepared him pancakes, quietly, so as not to wake him up. She later quickly dressed and tiptoed gently towards the door.

"Hello? Hello?" There was no one in the room. She was gone. He has been served breakfast. He shook his head. "Where is she gone to? Will I ever see her again?" he asked himself. All the same, he was a happy man because she had taken the money he deliberately left her on the table, along with one of his shirts.

Walking down the aisle of the grocery shop, he picked up the ricotta cheese from the shelf. "I definitely have to prepare the same breakfast she cooked. At least then I would have something to keep her in my memory." He felt a sharp pain by his lower ribs, as if someone trying to get his attention had pinched him. He turned, but he was alone by the shelf. He felt the urge to race along the aisle without knowing why or what he was buying. Lifting his head, he saw the 'breakfast lady' just about to leave the shop. He immediately left everything behind and chased after her.

As she walked by the still pond, a thousand questions ran through her mind. Here she was now with a man who never wanted anything in return. *Is he the bird I wished for? But how could he love me this much?* In tears, she kept mulling over the thoughts. *Is it a dream or fantasy?*
She searched deep in her soul to find out if she deserved to be loved that much. "Nothing! Nothing! Nothing!" She muttered. Just as she was about to wipe her tears away, she felt James' warm hands on her face. He whispered gently into her ear. "I am not worth your tears. You deserve better. All I am asking is that you give me a chance to be the *better* that you deserve. It doesn't matter where you have been and what you have done. Even if in all the years of your life you have done everything wrong, you have the chance today to make everything right." She turned, looked into his eyes passionately, and kissed him.

The strife of life seems unending. Unending life is unfulfilled destiny. But a fulfilled destiny is an end in itself.

TEARS OF HOPE

As David lay on the hospital bed, he turned away from the wall that he had been staring at for the past twelve hours. He had been searching for the answers of a seemingly unsolvable puzzle. Around him he saw anxious faces that were desperately trying to understand his fate. The faces all seemed to say the same thing: what makes such a man do this? Is it fate or destiny? He leaned forward on the bed, glanced at the faces and tears filled his eyes as he told them his story.

On May 15, David met his parents - the first time he had seen them in two years - for his graduation ceremony; a day of pride and glory, of which every radiant reflection of the morning sun reminded him. He was the only student to achieve a distinction in the university since Crayford took the enviable prize ten years ago. David walked to the platform with such elegance and 'amour propre' as the chancellor handed him his certificate. All he had heard and believed about himself was that he was a man bound for greatness beyond the realms of understanding. He knew he possessed extreme intelligence and uniqueness, but it was a gift he could not comprehend.

He kissed his parents goodbye. They promised each other a

family gathering and an assurance of 'sticking together' from now on. Happiness written all over his face, he smiled as he watched them disappear into the distance.

On the night of the graduation celebration, almost all his friends were around dancing, drinking, snuggling. He realised the following morning just what a night of debauchery it had been. A celebrated night for a memorable occasion indeed!

Still in a dizzy state in the morning, he heard the phone ringing. He staggered out of bed and murmured something into the handset that even he could not comprehend. The voice on the phone belonged to the family doctor. Instantly, it was as if the alcohol in his blood stream had vaporised. He stood there numb and speechless at the news. He dropped the phone and fell down with a loud thud. He could hear Doctor Stein's muffled voice coming from the speaker on the receiver, attempting to reassure him in the midst of such a tragic loss. David hung up and hit the bottle once again. How could he not have asked them to stay, or even gone back to Minnesota with them? Either way, he would have saved them or even died with them. What was the point of having the highest credentials if you have no one to share your glory? Lots of regrets and questions ran through his mind. Was this the end of the road?

Still disorientated and unaware of his surroundings, all he could hear was the voice of the Reverend silently drifting through the cool breeze. "Ashes to ashes, dust to dust…" Tears filled everyone's eyes as they gazed at the coffin being slowly lowered into the grave. He tried to look for a comforting face, but found none. All he could see were tears.

Just as everyone was leaving, he felt a touch of comfort on his broad, hefty shoulder. "Be strong, David. Be strong. It's okay; it's not the end of the world. I am Mr. Palmer from Palmer and Associates, the biggest architecture firm on the East Coast. I have been searching for you all this while and am glad I have finally found you - though I did not expect to meet under these circumstances. Come to my office on Monday. I have personally reserved a position for you with all the fringe benefits you could ever ask for."

David stood there speechless, staring at him in disbelief. A glimpse of hope in the middle of this devastation! He managed a smile and thanked him with a humble handshake. He turned back to look at his parents' grave and whispered, "At least you have made me smile."

Through the window of the building, you could see the terrain, the still pond that offered sanctuary for the ducks and a view that could disarm any mind armed with a suicidal intent. David gave a deep sigh as he turned to glance through the files on his desk. "Life couldn't be better. I'm doing what I love and being paid for it - with all the fringe benefits a man could ask for-" he said to himself.

As he drove through the lonely streets in his Mercedes S-Class, the phone in his car rang. "David, I am assigning you as the head of the biggest project we have ever had in our company's history," Mr. Palmer's voice echoed through the phone. He pondered how vehemently he would support and appraise the project.

As he went through the final project plan, he discovered his assistant had misplaced a metric measurement. However, making the necessary change would mean that he was supposed to be there to supervise the project development himself. A responsibility which, legally and within the bounds of company policy, he could delegate. He quickly hit the phone and got in touch with Mr.

Pliable. "I have made some rectifications on the final plan and I need you to get it from the office so you can incorporate them into the original plan," he said. "After all, he is as efficient as I am," David muttered to himself.

At the club, Mr. Pliable danced carelessly and drunk himself into a stupor. He could not resist the temptation, placed before him by his friends, to go to the club. When he got back home, he realised he was not ready to decimate his ecstatic sensation. *After all, I can amend the project in the morning,* he thought.

In the morning, he forgot all about what he'd been asked to do, and submitted the unchanged building plans. Realising his negligence, but not prepared to admit it, he assured the company of the certainty of the design. David, trusting Mr. Pliable, brushed over the idea of checking them again himself.

A few months into the project they realised the flaws in the design. The construction work that had already been done would have to be demolished, and building it again would cost the company millions as well as their reputation. Mr. Palmer was prepared to absorb the cost because David was such an asset. The board, on the contrary, was not prepared to risk their reputation, and their final decision was that David had to go.

David realised this could signal the end of his job, as soon as he saw Mr. Palmer's face as he emerged from the board meeting. "What is happening or what is going to happen?" he asked himself. He returned to his office to wait for a decision. The phone rang. His fears had become a reality. He looked out of the window, but this time he was sure the terrain would not dissuade him of his intent.

In that lonely park, he laid in his vomit, surrounded by flies, and many bottles of whisky. "Nothing left for me now except to drink myself to death. If only it will kill me, then let it be, what do I have to lose?" he shrugged. He tried to remember something nice, but all he could remember was the tears and the voice of the Reverend saying "Dust to dust…"

He turned on his back and hugged his shoulders so he could 'sleep to death.' When he opened his eyes, he saw a dazzling face that radiated grace, the intensity of which defied description.

"Hi, my name is Elena," she said. He shook his head to try to wake up from the 'dream' that was awakening his deeper emotions. "I found you sleeping in the park last night so I brought you home," she smiled. Still not able to distinguish reality from fantasy, he stretched out his hand, groping for more whisky so he could at least return to his deep sleep, but unfortunately caught a smooth, soft, feminine hand. She gave him a caress on his hand that invoked comfort and hope.

Some dreams are reality; his mother had once told him. They married after a year of love and fulfilment. David and Elena would sit up every night discussing their life and future prospects. He had at last found meaning in life. To love and be loved! He would mull over this thought in his head anytime he slid on the bed to sleep at night.

Soon Elena was pregnant with their first son. David would go to his parents' grave every weekend to tell them how he would be a good father, be there for his son, and make them proud. He could never hide his exultation. He had thought he would never know such love, peace and fulfilment again, but he thought wrong. He would make plans with Elena for their son; envisioning his son's bright future surrounded by love and affection.

On that fateful or faithful day, as Elena screamed in the delivery room, all he prayed for was to be a happily blessed man. After a few hours, the doctor came out with a face that David could hardly comprehend. He rushed to him and asked, "Doctor, how is my wife and baby?"

"David," he sighed, "Congratulations, you are now a father to a healthy baby boy." David, still not content, enquired, "Sure, I know, but how is my wife?" The doctor shook his head and said, "David, be a man as you hear this news. Please brace yourself. I am sorry. We did all our best but…"

All the people in the hospital could hear a man that was screaming out of his soul. "Why? Why? Are my sins so great they cannot be forgiven?" He clung on to the doctor and cried with such emotion that the doctor could not help but join him in tears. He touched David's right shoulder and whispered, "David, God gives life and takes life. If we accept one from him, would we not accept the other from him? Everything He does is for a reason. Enjoy your son but also try and honour your wife."

David accepted life as it was. He was blessed to have Junior. Junior had a smile that always reflected David's late father. He could clearly see the soul and life of his father in Junior. But his dislike for the theory of reincarnation meant his son could not possibly possess his father's soul. Every night, in the peak of the night, he would walk quietly to Junior's room and stare at him as he reminisced on the plans he had made with Elena.

"As long as I live, I will make sure even with my last breath, that Junior achieves all that Elena had planned. I live for him and he lives for Elena and my father. I made them a promise," he said.

He would go to the park where Elena had found him, not to drink himself to death, but to celebrate the best time of his life with

Junior. Everyone at the park would congregate around the boy and express how adorable he was. It always helped him to forget the tragedy.

One night, Junior had a high fever. David did all he could to administer first aid but to no avail. Junior kept on screaming and crying violently. After giving him some medicine, he tried reheating food for Junior in the kitchen. The food was on the stove when the son fell into a breathless trance.

"Gracious, what is happening to him?" David left the kitchen and raced as fast as he could to the hospital. He sat by his son, watching him 'sleep' in a coma. Should he pray? Will he find refuge and salvation for him and his son?

After about thirty minutes, the doctor called him aside and asked him to go home for some rest. He sensed something was not right in the tone of the doctor's voice. "Is he alright? Is he coming back to me?" Words could not describe the emotions and reactions of a man who has seen this scenario before and witnessed the outcome. He immediately broke into tears. The doctor did everything he could to comfort him but nothing seemed good enough to console David. He had lost Junior.

David, in no fit state to drive, allowed the doctor to escort him home. As they turned at the end of the street they saw fire-fighters at David's house trying to put out a blazing fire. In his haste to get to the hospital, he had forgotten to turn off the stove in the kitchen. He could not cry anymore. Tears would not make things right. He'd had enough. Finally, the thought of death was the only relief.

He walked to a nearby pharmacy and bought a bottle of poison. "This is it!" he said to himself. "Dust to dust…" Lost in his thoughts he failed to see a car coming along the lonely road. He was hit by the car, which sent him flying into the bushes as the driver struggled to apply his brakes.

The driver stopped, ran quickly towards David but, much to the driver's amazement, David was up on his feet walking as if nothing had happened. "What?" The driver exclaimed. He helped David to his car and drove him home.

The driver, who was a psychologist, saw the poison in David's hand and realised what he was contemplating. For the next two months, David underwent intensive counselling in the hands of one of the world's most famous psychologists.

At last, he had found the help and trust of a friend he needed: somebody to talk to, who could understand him, and who was well equipped to assist him through life. He was becoming a man again with hope for the future. All is not lost, he realised.

One day, while the counsellor was absent, his new best friend's short, slender and blue-eyed wife came to David in a plain white nightgown that revealed every inch of her curves. She wiggled her hips at him and walked towards him. At first he thought it was just pity and affection, but she demanded more. David thought, *I have enough sins that I am still paying for and besides, I will never breach the trust of my friend.* He carefully pushed her aside and walked out of the living room. In shame and fear, the wife implicated David in forcefully violating her. What? Who was there? How can he prove otherwise? His friend would not listen to him and supported his wife in her allegation.

Sentenced for a decade, which for David seemed like a century, he was made to work long hours of manual labour by the prison guards. The sadistic guards would single David out and make life hard for him in the penitentiary. As a sign of pity, his friend recommended regular attention, as David was clearly suicidal. That did not eliminate the humiliation, the emotional and psychological torture for ten years. Every night he would hear the resounding words by his parents' grave. As if calling out, 'David, come home'.

One bright afternoon, a guard walked to his cell and shouted in such a disgruntled voice, "Hey, man, come out. It's time." David had lost track of time in the long dark hall. At last, he was due to be released. He wished he could spend all his life in the prison. What life and hope was he going out there for? To where? To whom?

Walking down the street in front of the prison, he definitely knew that this time, if he had to go, he had to do it right.

As he stood on the fiftieth floor, his whole life flashed before him. Dozens of questions ran through his mind. *What have I lived for? Why am I still alive? What did I do to deserve all this? Is it worth bearing the cross of innocence, or wearing the cloak of guilt? I guess I will never live to find out! It's enough! It's enough! It's all over this time.* He let himself fall to the ground. He felt a surge of pain on his backbone and instantly passed out.

David had fallen into a truckload of bed cushions heading towards the new hospital. He was discovered by the doctors immediately, and sent to the emergency room. He had lived.

Finishing his story, all he could see was a gathering of the whole hospital around his bed with tears in their eyes. Once again, he was seeing tears.

He turned back to the wall and whispered, "I think I now understand. Behind every tear, lies a glimpse of hope."

Sometimes the necessary thing to do to overcome evil is to do nothing.

THE TENDERNESS OF LOVE

I

The clock ticked. Lucy Jeffney, a devoted housewife, quickly got up from her bed as she banged on the timer. She ran into her children's room and woke them up.

"Come on kids, time to get up for school," she said.

She took Juanita to the bathroom and started washing her. Nick, the eldest of the children walked around, hopelessly trying to find his books. Though he had kept himself in impeccable health, and was extra cautious with his image, he never seemed to put his books in order.

"Nick, are you okay?" Lucy asked.

"No, mom, I don't like going to school. Miss Moore never lets me talk in class. She always allows Jimmy to answer all the questions."

"Don't worry, Nick. Sometimes, when we are quiet, it shows how wise we are. You need to know that."

He shrugged and buried himself in his stash of books.

Juanita stood by the drawer desperately riffling through her clothes. "Mom, can I have new socks? Please!" she pleaded. "Sure honey, I will get you a pair from my drawer."

"Thank you," she responded.

At the breakfast table, Lucy motioned for the family to bow their heads.

"Thank you for this morning and the food. Amen," she prayed and they all responded, "Amen." Nick began his long speech about school, but Lucy interrupted him, "Nick, honey, never talk with your mouth full."

"Yes - because you can get choked," Juanita chimed in. She got up from her chair and raced towards her lunch box. Nick took one last bite of his toast and picked up his school bag, hesitant to join the others in the rush to the family car.

Danny Jeffney, a successful building contractor, kissed the children and Lucy goodbye and hurried to his Jaguar. He sped off from the garage and down the deserted street. At his destination, he walked into his office building, tossing his head carelessly with contentment. He reached the reception and greeted Wendy, who was dressed in a brown shirt that perfectly complemented her blonde hair.

"Any calls or messages? Did the secretary of housing call about the new proposal?" he asked.

"No, sir," Wendy replied.

He turned towards his office but, looking back, smiled and said, "And oh, by the way, that's a lovely shirt. It really fits you."

"Thank you, sir."

Danny smiled and closed the door behind him. He tapped his keyboard and began sorting out his emails. He turned to the files on the desk and patiently read through them. After about two hours, he picked up his coat and walked out of his office.

"Wendy, if I get any business calls tell them I am off to the construction site."

"Yes, sir. And if your wife calls..?" she asked.

"Tell her I will be home at the usual time."

Danny stood by the half-completed building structure talking with the supervisor and his workers. He had always found it more productive to spend more time at the construction site than in his office. He had been blessed with a new secretary who adequately understood his business and could handle any problems that arose in his absence.

With the house to clean and dinner to prepare, Lucy's day sped past. It was 4.00pm and a mad dash to pick up the kids from school ensued. "Hi Nick. Hi Juan," she said to them as she sped off.

Wendy was busily scheduling Danny's appointments when the phone rang.

"Hello, this is Dan & Luc construction. How may I help you?"

"Where is Mr. Jeffney?"

"I am sorry, sir, Mr. Jeffney left for the construction site, but I am sure he is at home at this time. You could try his cell phone."

"Yeah, I tried but there was no response."

"Can I take a message, sir?"

"Yes. Tell him Mr. Peterson called and that I will be expecting him at the meeting."

"Will certainly do, sir. Thank you," said Wendy.

Peterson understood immediately why Danny was not at the office at that time: he was definitely running home to Lucy's spaghetti and crabmeat.

Danny would have liked the opportunity to choose what meals he had, but always found it difficult because it didn't matter what flavour a food had, Lucy could turn it into a mouth-watering delicacy.

Danny sounded his horn as he entered the garage. Nick and Juanita ran out enthusiastically to meet him. "Hey, how are you doing?" he patted Nick on the back and placed Juanita on his shoulders. Lucy came out from the kitchen and kissed him. She took his briefcase into the bedroom and came back to set the table for dinner.

"Honey, if you keep on cooking like this, I bet I will never leave home for work again," Danny enthused, receiving support from the smiles and nods of his family.

Lucy went up to Nick's room after dinner and said, "Nick, please do remember to ask God to watch over you, okay." She loved to give them the assurance of the watchful eye of the big man upstairs. "If Danny and I can't be there all the time, better give them someone who will be there for them always," she would say.

"Okay, Mom. Good night."

"Good night, Nick."

She raced back to Juanita's room and bent over to kiss her. "And you too, my little angel. Don't forget to pray."

"Okay, Mom. Good night," Juanita said, easing her grips on Lucy.

"Honey, I am really thankful for us and the kids," Lucy said. She came out of the en suite bathroom, turned the sheets and sat on the bed. "They are really a blessing. Nick's doing well at school! And Juan is so polite and respectful!"

"Oh, honey, I love you. Thank you."

Danny laughed. "No, thank you instead. And I love you, too."

She smiled, kissed him and turned off the bedside lamp.

"Good night," Danny said, as he rolled over onto the bed.

II

"Hey, honey, what do you think about inviting Wendy, my new secretary, over for lunch this weekend?" Danny asked, pouring himself a cup of coffee. "She has been doing such an amazing job at the office, and I think it would be nice for the family to know her more. She is really a good person and I think the kids, especially Juan, will like her."

"I don't know, but if you think its right, I have no objection," Lucy replied, showing little interest in the proposition. Juanita sat there with wide-open eyes. "Mommy, please. I want new friends. Please can she come around?" she asked.

"Wendy is not a Barbie. Hey Barbie, are you hungry?" Nick teased in Juanita's voice.

"Stop it, Nick. It's not good to make fun of people," said Lucy.

"Sorry Mom, but I don't know if she will like me too," Nick said, turning his face away.

"Come on, Nick. Why do you say that?" Danny enquired.

"Honey, you seem to forget that Nick is shy with the ladies. Anyway, I guess it's okay to invite her home," Lucy concurred. "Well, I don't have lots of trusted friends, so maybe I am about to have one," she smiled. Danny was busy reading the morning newspaper. He took a last sip of coffee and jumped off his feet, kissing them and heading for the garage.

As Danny approached Wendy's desk, he asked, "Any messages?" He usually got worried when his cell phone remained silent after office hours. There were times when he had to answer the secretary's call as early as 3am, so he knew that business could be negotiated at any time of the day or night.

"Yes, sir. Mr. Peterson called yesterday. He said he will be expecting you at the meeting."

"Ah, I have been expecting his call. I will have to call him later," he smiled with his eyes sparkling in excitement.

"Sir, are you okay?" she asked.

"Sure, couldn't be any better. Peterson is my childhood friend. We started school together. Well, right through to the university. In fact, we were roommates as well. We go a long way back." He shook his head, smiling.

Wendy stared in surprise. "Really, sir?"

"Oh, yes," he replied with a deep insisting voice. He moved closer to Wendy's desk, stared shortly, and opened his mouth to say something to her. He stopped, raised his right hand in the air, and turned.

"Never mind," he said, and walked to his office still shaking his head.

Danny switched on his computer. Within minutes, a small noise signalled the arrival of a new mail. He read the name of the sender and leaned forward. He pushed his chair back, threw his hands in the air and exhaled deeply.

"Wow. This is the dream," he said. He looked up and said, "Big man, if you are up there, help me achieve this dream. He turned to the phone. "I need to call Pete."

Andy, the odd job man, pushed the lawn mower across the lawn recklessly, singing in tune to his Walkman and nodding his head as he worked happily. Lucy could not help but wonder how he was able to cut any grass at all. Andy was working like a professional but acting like a fool. Lucy knelt by her new flowerbed, watering the young new shoots of roses. She loved roses. They always reminded her of her Aunt Doris.

Celeste, Lucy's neighbour, came out of her house waving to Lucy. The sound of the lawn mower drowned out her faint voice. Lucy looked up and saw her waving. She quickly got up on her feet and waved back. "Andy, can you please switch the machine off for a minute?" Lucy insisted. "Thank you." She moved close to the hedges.

"Could you please tell that noisy man to turn that down? I'm trying to catch a nap," Celeste requested.

"Sorry, Celeste. It's just for a few minutes. He will finish in no time," Lucy said, convincingly, but she could not help feeling guilty for waking up the poor old woman. Celeste turned. "Then I might as well get to the kitchen to bake some cookies. Juanita might come over this evening for some."

"Oh, Celeste, that's very kind. You don't have to. But anyway, thank you."

She turned back to Andy and said, "You can carry on, but be sure not to take too long with it, okay!" She resumed watering the red and white roses in the garden.

Andy went behind the hedges and began designing a caricature of Juanita's cat, Rufus. He was an expert at that, and could design any kind of animal with the right kind of hedge plants. "I am sure the Jeffrey's love my work because of this," he said to himself as he patiently trimmed the hedges into the shape of a cat.

Inside the house, the phone began to ring. Lucy walked quickly to answer it.

"Hello, honey," she said, recognising Danny's voice.

"Hi. Did Andy come over to do the garden?"

"Yes. We are still working on it."

"Great. Tell him not to forget to design Juan's cat…"

"Oh sure," Lucy interrupted.

Danny continued. "Otherwise she will be very disappointed; she's been looking forward to showing it to her new friend."

"Ah yes, Wendy's visit this weekend. I'm sure Juan will be happy to see her," said Lucy.

"Good to hear that. So, honey, what's for dinner?"

She smiled. "Something special. If I tell you, it will not be a surprise anymore."

Danny paused as he saw someone open his office door. "Honey, I gotta go. See you at dinner. Bye."

He embraced Pete, who was smiling as broadly as ever, with open arms.

"Hey, pal. It's about time," said Danny.

"Time! When you are having fun on the phone with Lucy. You two love birds!"

"How did you know?"

"Lucky guess."

"Then this time you hit the jackpot," said Danny. They both laughed and sat down.

"So, Dan, at last, huh?"

"Sure thing. You could say that. I just got the message from Carl."

"But it's not officially announced!" said Pete.

"Come on, Pete. You are talking as if you don't know Carl. The only thing he'll not do is let us have an upper hand in the bidding."

"I know. His 'fairness' speech…" Pete chimed in.

"We have to make sure there is no corruption in the system," Danny spoke in a deep voice, mimicking Carl's. They both laughed loudly as they exclaimed, "And it should start from us, the individuals."

"You know it, Dan. Let us do everything possible to secure this contract. As for the financing, I am all up for it…"

"I know, 'Mr. Cash'," Danny teased. "Well, I'll need to start the paperwork right away. Get in touch with the secretary and all the necessary parties before the bidding." Wendy walked into the office. "Sir, here are the files you requested," she said.

"Thank you, Wendy."

Pete turned to her, and lowered the bridge of his spectacles down his nose. "Hello lady!" he said, winking at Wendy, and throwing a kiss in the air.

Wendy giggled and looked at him with an inquiring face.

"Don't mind him, Wendy. He is just admiring," Danny said, gesturing to Wendy that that would be all.

She turned to leave but stopped and asked, "Sir, is this Mr. Peterson?"

"Well, the last time I checked," Pete responded.

"Really? It's nice to meet you finally. Mr. Jeffney has told me a lot about you," Wendy said, feeling more comfortable and confident this time.

"All good things, I hope," he said, looking at Danny.

Pete stretched out his hand and took Wendy's in his. He gently placed a kiss on it. "The pleasure is all mine."

"Well, I will talk to you later, sir," she said.

"Hey, pal. Back to business," Danny said.

"Sure, sure, sure," Pete turned to him.

"Pal, I am not scared about the money. I know you are good for it."

"We're gonna nail this," they said, in unison.

"This time, I am sure Dennis and his associates will not have a chance at it," said Danny.

"How about we bring in our political friends?" Pete asked.

"Hmmm. That's a good idea. Well, we will start preparing. But for now, I gotta run. I can smell Lucy's lasagne with extra cheese," Danny said, prompting laughter from both of them.

Danny sat on the bed at home with a book in his hands. "Honey, I am about to make a move that will change our future forever. And I mean *forever*," he said.

Lucy leapt up from the bed with surprise. "What is it? Tell me. I am your wife."

"Don't worry. D&L is now at the incubating period. When the whole plan hatches, you will surely know. I promise."

"I can hardly wait, honey. You know I don't like too many surprises."

Danny leaned forward and took her chin in his hands. He looked deeply into her eyes and smiled. "It sometimes pays to wait. You'll see."

III

Lucy felt very happy. She could not tell if it was the early morning brightness of the sun promising a glorious day or the anticipation of waiting for Danny to reveal his hidden agenda. She smiled broadly as she poured coffee into Danny's mug. *Life doesn't get much better than this*, she thought as she and Danny enjoyed the children's lively chatter. Nick's face beamed with excitement, full of information and enthusiasm on the nutritional value of their breakfast.

The Peterson family sat behind their breakfast table. They normally had breakfast early on Saturdays but this time Linz had changed the timer so they could have a little more time in bed. "Well, sometimes it is good to have enough rest," she would say. Their children, Piper and Ruby, pleaded desperately to go to the Jeffneys'. Pete smiled, got up and reached for the phone.

"Okay, everyone, Uncle Pete and the family are coming over for lunch," Danny said, placing the handset on the kitchen table.

Juanita jumped in glee but Nick turned to look away.

"That's great, honey, because Wendy is also coming here today," Lucy said, smiling happily.

"Yes, it's perfect timing!" Danny said.

"Nick, why the long face?" he asked.

"Well, all they - Piper, Ruby and Juan - will do is to watch cartoons and I can't play my games. I will have to sit down and not have anything interesting to do," Nick replied.

"Don't worry, Nick. I will get you something to do," Danny said, patting his back.

Nick smiled approvingly. "Sure. Okay."

"Sorry guys, I need to hurry up for shopping," Lucy said, walking out from the kitchen.

Half an hour later, as she pushed the heavy trolley, she realised she had bought way too much food and drink, but she told herself it would be worth it.

Danny and Nick sat behind the television, playing Nick's PlayStation. They kept challenging each other as they urged their players on, Danny trying as hard as he could, intermittently screaming with enthusiasm. Beside them sat Juanita, happily playing with her dolls and her cat Rufus. At the familiar sound of the Peterson's horn, Juanita jumped to her feet.

"Dad, they are here," she said, and ran towards the door. Unable to unlock the door with her feeble hands, Nick came to her aid, before quickly returning to his game.

"Hi Juan. How are you? You are really growing big each day," Linz said, smiling as she touched the girl's shoulder. Juanita rushed to embrace Piper, who was struggling to push her toys into her backpack. They jumped, kept giggling and exchanging words that the 'adults' couldn't comprehend.

Danny and Nick detached themselves from their fun and headed for the door.

"Hi Nick," Ruby said, waving. Nick returned a smile. Danny

gave the girls a pat on the back and gestured for them to go inside the house.

"Hey, pal," said Pete, as he shook hands with Danny.

"You look good today, Dan. What's up?"

"Nothing much, Pete. Just trying to beat Nick at his game."

"Wooh, be careful. He is a clever kid. Don't say I didn't warn ya!" They both laughed as they walked into the house.

Linz had already served herself a cup of tea, and enquired, "Where is the lady of the house?" Juanita quickly raised her hands trying to get attention. Linz bent down towards her and said, "That's sweet, Juan. But I mean the big lady." Danny responded, "She's gone out shopping."

"Oh no! If we had been here earlier I could have gone with her!" Linz exclaimed, regret in her eyes.

"Don't worry, she'll be back very soon," Danny said.

Linz turned back to the kitchen to get herself another cup of tea. Pete called out. "Honey, can you get me a cup of water?"

"Sure, sweetheart, just a minute," she responded.

Pete turned to Danny who had crossed his legs on the sofa. "Pal, can you get the race on? Where is the remote?" he asked.

Danny got up from his seat, picked the remote from the top of the game console and tossed it over to Pete. He carefully picked up the consoles and arranged them on the perfectly crafted side table.

"Nick, could you come down and help Mommy get the groceries from the car?" Danny shouted, hearing the sound of Lucy's horn in the driveway.

"Okay, Dad," Nick responded, running down the stairs.

Linz walked to the door and opened it. She saw Lucy trying to fit many grocery bags into her arms. "Come on Lucy. Let me give you a hand. You don't have to carry all the bags," she said, and smiled.

"Thank you, Linz. Have you been here for long?"

"Not really. Everyone is having fun, though. Well, everyone except me," Linz said.

Lucy, relieved of the shopping bags, rested her arms. "Ah, the boys are at it again, huh?" she asked, and smiled.

"Sure yes, you can say that again," Linz responded, and they both chuckled.

Nick walked into the kitchen with the last bag.

"Nick, how about some nutritional advice? What is good to cook?" Linz asked, smiling at him.

Nick gave her an embarrassing smile and shook his head. "Sorry, but I am busy playing games with Ruby," he responded.

"Sure, go have fun," Lucy urged him.

Danny and Pete sat calmly on the sofa, reminiscing about old times. They loved to share thoughts on their life at school. Pete's vivid recollections of almost all the negligible and weird events always provided new topics for discussions.

"Yeah, the old school days!" said Pete, rolling his eyeballs, revealing a little embarrassment.

"Wow, it was really amazing. You know sometimes I miss University." Danny sat up with interest.

Pete began laughing.

"Do you remember Marty?"

Danny lay back, trying to figure out if his subconscious mind would register that name.

"So, what are we preparing?" Linz asked Lucy, as she unloaded the last grocery bag onto the table in the kitchen.

"Good question," Lucy replied. "In fact it's something special. Very different. It's called Koulibiac, with a honey sauce."

"Really?" said Linz, her eyes wide open in surprise.

"Yes. Do you remember Aunt Doris?" Lucy asked.

Linz, placing her forefinger on her chin, murmured, "Hmm, I guess so."

Lucy's face beamed with excitement. Her fixation on the pan in her hands intensified and she said, "Aunt Doris would always prepare this sauce with roasted potatoes anytime she came to visit us when we were kids."

"That's interesting. Is it her recipe?" Linz asked.

"I am not too sure. She said she got it from an African friend. I cannot remember specifically, but I think from one of the African villages. She said the locals there reckon that honey is good for a child's mental development."

Linz sneered. "I guess I need to ask Doctor Nick to confirm that!"

"Yeah, yeah. I now remember," said Danny, getting up from the sofa. "He used to date all the girls because he was, like, the lion king."

"Exactly!" Pete affirmed. "And he even tried asking Mandy out for a date."

"Mandy?" Danny exclaimed, aghast.

Pete nodded.

"But, Mandy was… was… like Mother Teresa on campus."

"I know, but Marty made a bet with his friends that he could take Mandy out for a date," said Pete.

Danny began laughing uncontrollably.

"Hold on Danny, the most interesting bit is yet to come. He approached Mandy in front of everyone and, you know, made his move, but he kept on panting for words. He couldn't say what he wanted to…"

"Wow, that guy had guts," Danny interrupted.

"So," Pete continued, "Mandy was kinda surprised and shy so she looked down and around, and everyone was standing there with their jaws dropped. Finally, she replied, with a little bit of concern in her voice, by reciting Matthew 7:7."

"No way!" Danny yelled.

"Yes. Yes. So, the guy got really ticked off and abused her as revenge," Pete continued, still laughing.

"Oh, no", said Danny, covering his face with his hands.

Pete suppressed his laughter and continued, "So the guy went home and asked his younger brother. 'Hey, buddy, what's in Matthew 7:7?' His brother looked at him and replied, 'Ask and it shall be given to you.'"

"No way!" Danny exclaimed.

Pete continued, nodding. "The guy then looked at himself in the mirror, and cursed himself."

"Look, Lucy, this might be her," said Linz, pointing out to the driveway.

"Great. Right on time. The food is almost done."

Linz headed towards the door but took a detour into the living room. The boys were still laughing at their jokes.

"Hey guys, what are you discussing? Women or horses?" Linz asked.

Pete and Danny became silent for a few seconds. Then Pete responded, "Both."

Danny stared at Pete, puzzled.

"Yes, yes. We are talking about mares," said Pete.

"Mares?" Linz scoffed.

Pete and Danny turned at each other and collapsed into hysteria.

Wendy rang the doorbell. Linz was instantly startled because of the allusions from the boys' pranks. "I will get it," she said, walking to the door.

Linz offered a warm smile.

"Hello, Mrs. Jeffney. I am Wendy."

"Well, well. What do we have here? Your name matches your face." Linz paused.

"Hmmm, sorry! I am Mrs. Peterson but please come in," she said.

"Hey guys, she is here," Linz shouted.

Pete and Danny stopped laughing. "Hello Wendy. Welcome. Make yourself at home," both said, at the same time.

Wendy gave an appreciative smile, "Hello sir, hello Mr. Peterson," she replied.

Linz interrupted. "Let's leave these gentlemen be. They are having their own fun. We'll have ours in the kitchen," Linz held Wendy's arm and led her out of the living room.

Wendy was a bit startled by the large, well-designed and spotless kitchen. She managed to compose herself and tried not to reveal her deeper admiration. She wanted to be careful not to send any mixed signals on her first visit.

"Hello Mrs. Jeffney," she said, just as she got to the kitchen.

"Hi, Wendy. Welcome to our home. How are you?" said Lucy, dimples appearing in the smooth contours of her face.

"I am fine, thank you, ma'am."

"Don't be silly, Wendy. Just call me Lucy," she waved at her.

"Wow, you have an amazing house," Wendy said.

"Thank you Wendy. Mr. Jeffney designed it himself. But never mind that, he has been telling us lots about you," said Lucy.

"Well, I hope he was complimentary," Wendy said, with a smile that betrayed her embarrassment.

"Only that you have impeccable standards," said Lucy, smiling.

"Okay girls, I guess the food is done now. Linz, can you please set the table?"

Wendy placed her handbag on the countertop. "Can I help, Mrs. Jeffney, err… Lucy?" she asked.

"Sure you can. That is if you don't mind," Lucy replied.

The boys sat down quietly, having returned to a controlled state.

Pete turned to Danny. "Hey pal, what are the ladies doing in there? I am starving."

"Well, let's take a peep," Danny said, as they both got up and headed to the kitchen.

"Is it ready yet? I'm starving," Pete said.

Linz turned to Wendy. "Don't worry, it's his game."

Lucy smiled and said, "Come on Linz, leave the boys alone."

Danny, standing by the door, waved his hand in the air and said, "Yeah, come on ladies, give us some credit, will you?"

"Kids, lunch is ready!" Lucy shouted, walking up the stairs.

"Okay, Mom." They all responded in a resounding voice.

Juanita quickly ran up to Lucy and asked, "Mom, is Wendy here?"

"Sure, sweetheart. You will like her. Trust me."

"Linz, can you say grace for us?" Lucy asked her after everyone had sat down at the table.

Pete cleared his throat and smiled, looking up at Linz.

"Let us pray," Linz asked for their attention, shaking her head. "Thank you for this food and always make our homes happy. Amen."

"Amen," they all responded.

Lucy got up to start serving but Danny reprimanded her. "Honey, please serve the kids and allow the grown-ups to do justice to this irresistible meal."

"Sure, honey," Lucy responded, and began serving the children.

Wendy sat down, shy and reluctant to serve herself. Linz noticed her expression of discomfort. She said to her, "Come on, Wendy. Feel free to help yourself with the food. Or is it because your boss is around?"

Wendy covered her mouth and laughed sheepishly. She got up and dug into the steamy hot Koulibiac.

"So, Wendy, for how long have you been working for D&L?" Linz asked.

"For about four months, ma'am."

"Please, drop this 'ma'am' stuff! Just Linz."

They all burst into laughter. Wendy shifted her gaze from Danny in embarrassment.

The three little girls kept on giggling to themselves. They were so consumed in their chat that they weren't at all distracted by the personal conversations of the adults. At least, they had been taught not to meddle in the conversations of adults and they seemed to be perfectly adhering to that teaching.

"I tell you, guys. Wendy is really an asset at the office. She redesigned the database. I now have all my important data stored electronically," said Danny.

Wendy tilted her eyes in embarrassment. "Well it's my job."

"That's excellent work, Wendy. Keep it up," Lucy said.

"I guess, he can now transfer some of his work home and stay in to enjoy Lucy's recipes," Linz said, laughing.

"You can say that again!" Pete chimed in.

Wendy finally lifted her head – she had her face downwards most of the time - and glanced at the children.

"So, what names can I put to these lovely faces?" She pointed to the kids.

"Sorry Wendy, I should have introduced everyone before… "

Linz interrupted, "I guess the food was the priority, huh?"

"Well," Lucy continued, "This is Pete, Danny's twin brother – although not by birth."

"Oh, yes. I have already met him at the office," said Wendy.

"Really? He didn't hit on you, did he?" Linz asked.

"Yes, Pete's a charmer - a real ladies' man," Lucy affirmed.

Pete blushed at the praises. He knew his prowess and charm with women, but coming from those two ladies, he surely loved it.

"This is Nick, our son. Next to him is Juan, our last child. Over the other side is Ruby, Pete and Linz's first daughter."

Danny interrupted politely. "She's our computer whiz."

Ruby lifted her head with pride. Lucy continued, "And lastly, Piper, their second daughter."

Pete smiled. "Our future high court judge," he said.

Linz stared at Pete and waved her hands in the air. "But if she turns into Judge Schneider, I will definitely make her change her profession," she retorted.

"No, why do you say that? It's a noble profession," said Wendy.

"Maybe you haven't heard the story. They say he is so strict with the law that he actually sent his mother to court for abandoning his father, whilst they were still married," Linz said, firmly.

"Come on, Linz. It's just hearsay. There is no proof," said Pete.

Linz flared up in anger, looking at Pete sternly and defensively.

"Please, everyone. Can we just finish eating? We can discuss life afterwards," Lucy pleaded.

The room became quiet for some time, with everyone busy, either gnawing their food or refraining from inciting any further disagreement.

Juanita kept staring intensely at Wendy. She called out to Lucy and said, "Mom, I want to go."

"Sure, sweetheart, I will take you," said Lucy, getting up from her chair.

"Can she go with me?" said Juanita, pointing at Wendy.

"No, Juan. Wendy is still eating," said Lucy.

"It's okay, Lucy. I can go with her. Well, if you don't mind." "No, sure you can go with her!" said Lucy, smiling.

As Juanita and Wendy left the table, Danny glanced at Lucy, trying to gauge her reaction at having a stranger in the house.

"Wendy! Juan likes you," Linz shouted behind them just before they got to the door.

"That's Juan. She likes everyone," Pete chimed in.

"Well, it's in the blood," Linz said.

"Really, she is a nice lady," said Lucy.

"Sure, yes. She is. I bear testimony to that," said Pete, with a smile.

Linz stared intensely at Pete, her mouth wide open.

"What? I just agree," Pete shrugged.

"Mom, I am finished," Nick said.

"Yeah. Me too," said Ruby and Piper.

"Sure, but please wait for dessert," said Lucy.

"And what is for dessert?" Pete asked, with a curious face.

"Well, its nectarine dessert cake with whipped cream," said Lucy.

"Wow, I can't wait to dig in," Pete said.

Lucy and Linz cleared the used plates. Pete pushed his chair backwards a little, and turned to the two women. "That was a lovely meal," he said. "It was completely irresistible."

They all nodded in agreement. Pete kept on rubbing his hands on his belly.

Wendy and Juanita came back from the bathroom. Juanita let go of Wendy's hand, smiled, and said, "Thank you."

"You are welcome," Wendy tickled her chin.

Pete took a bite of his dessert and nodded. "Wow, this is so delicious. Is it one of your recipes?" he asked Lucy.

"No. This one is a popular dessert," Lucy replied.

Linz became restless for not saying much and quickly interrupted. "So, Wendy, what time does Danny leave the office?"

Danny turned to look at Wendy, wondering what she was going to say.

"Hmm. About five o'clock in the evening," Wendy replied.

"I see," said Pete. "Then I guess he always uses fifteen minutes instead of the normal half an hour rushing home for…" he paused, and moved his eyes downwards towards his plate.

"Come on, guys, let's involve Wendy in the fun. It should not be only me," Danny said.

Nick, who had been silent the whole time he had been at the table, finally spoke. "Mom, can I have more cream?" Wendy smiled at Nick. Lucy turned to Wendy and said, "Oh, Wendy, its just that he's usually shy around ladies."

Wendy smiled, "But he is cute though. I guess he is popular with the girls at school."

Nick turned in embarrassment as Lucy served him more cream.

"Okay, now I am done," said Pete.

"Likewise," Danny said.

"Thank you for the lovely meal, ladies," Pete and Danny said as they headed to the living room.

The children followed suit, running happily upstairs into their playroom.

"Can I help clear the table?" Wendy offered. Lucy waved to Wendy. "No, you just leave it to us," she smiled appreciatively. Lucy was good at making people understand her thoughts about them.

The three women headed to the kitchen, giggling with content at the boys' compliments. Lucy and Linz sat down, patiently listening as Wendy talked at length about life at the office. Juanita rushed into the kitchen and grabbed Wendy's hand. She looked at her, smiled and asked "Can you please help me put the diaper on my Barbie?"

"Sure, Juanita. Where is it?" Wendy asked.

"In my room," Juanita replied, pointing upstairs.

Wendy turned to Lucy and asked, "Lucy, is it okay to go upstairs with her?"

"Yeah, sure. Feel free to go around."

"Thank you," she said, heading upstairs with Juanita.

When they had left the kitchen, Linz smiled at Lucy and said, "Wow, Juan is hooked to her already."

"Yeah, I know. Isn't it amazing?" said Lucy.

Pete spread himself on the sofa in the living room. He sighed, yawned and unbuckled his belt. "Pal, I am stuffed," he said.

"That's good," said Danny. "You can't tell any more jokes."

Rufus the cat was lying lazily on the sofa. Pete moved to sit comfortably on the sofa, and lifted the cat. "My God! What has she been feeding it?" he asked. "He is heavier than a block of stone." Danny began laughing. "That's exactly what happens when you eat and sleep but don't take any exercise. What do you expect? To be on the tracks?" He brushed his hair with his fingers.

"Oh yeah! The tracks. That reminds me. I've got last month's race on disc." Danny reached forward to the shelves beside the television. "Here it is," he said, as he pushed the disc in the deck.

After about half an hour, Pete looked at the clock, picked up his keys from the table and turned to Danny.

"Danny! I gotta go now."

"Really?"

"Yes. I have to get home and do one or two things before I sleep this evening. Don't worry. I will see you at the live race."

"Sure. It's really been great today," said Danny.

"Definitely! Definitely!" Pete said, as he headed for the kitchen.

"Ladies, are you done in the kitchen?" Pete asked. "I guess it's time to head back," he said.

"Well, we've just finished. We are just chatting," Linz responded. Linz turned to Lucy. "Alrighty then, Lucy. Thanks a lot for today. We should be going now."

Linz left the kitchen and headed upstairs, calling out to Ruby and Piper.

Wendy came out of Juanita's bedroom with Piper and Juanita. She had managed to acquaint herself with Juanita's friendly personality - although most of the work was done by Juanita herself. She smiled at Lucy and said, "Well, me too. I guess I should be on my way."

Juanita stood under the stairs. She waved at Wendy, and with a pleading voice and friendly gesture tried to convince Wendy to stay a little bit longer. It was obvious she had loved the temporary presence of her new friend but persuading her, she thought, might be pushing her luck. Wendy realised her effort but politely declined, assuring her of another visit. "We would love that." Lucy smiled.

"It was a pleasure having you around," said Lucy, shifting her eyes onto her daughter to show how particularly pleasurable it had been for Juanita. Both families laughed at the beautiful connection between Lucy and Wendy, pleading with Lucy to let Wendy leave, finally.

Lucy saw Nick trying to hide his face behind Danny. She carefully refrained from embarrassing him. But she still wanted him to say something to their new friend. "Come on, Nick, please try and say something to Wendy," she pleaded.

Nick came out from behind Danny, managed a smile and waved good-bye. Pleased, and made happy by the attentions of the young boy, Wendy waved back at him, returning his smile.

"She is amazing with kids," said Linz, looking at everyone's faces. They all nodded to concur, as the Petersons walked to their Jeep.

Linz turned to Ruby and Piper, trying to make sure they took all their toys with them. She knew they would be forced to drive back to the Jeffneys' if Piper were to leave her favourite Barbie doll behind. Piper always loved to sleep with the Barbie by her side. The two girls lifted their bags. "It's all in here", they said.

Pete shook hands with Danny. "Hey, pal. Be sure to be at the race!" he said. Pete never missed it, but Danny understood Pete's special interest in the forthcoming race.

The two women watched their spouses' enthusiastic display, and teased them. "Men and their hobbies," they exploded in laughter. The Jeffney's waved at the Petersons. They turned towards the house, happily and content with the day, and laughing with joy. Lucy touched Juanita on her shoulder. "So, you made a friend today!"

IV

The warm morning sun offered hope for some pleasurable outdoor activities. For the two race enthusiasts, it was a perfect opportunity for them to show their unflinching support for the favourite. Due to an injury, Ambrosino had been off the track for a month, but was now back to capture their hearts - though definitely not their wallets – once again. Their passion for the game was always rekindled when their favourite was on the course. Pete loved to display his passion and intelligence at the races. He turned to Danny and pointed at the horses, who were in their stalls and ready to start the race.

"Hey pal, have you seen number twelve? Ambrosino! He looks fit and ready for today's race." Danny sat up a little to have a look at their hero. Pete continued with such enthusiasm.

"Do you know why he always wins?" Danny laughed. "Oh, yes, I know. It's either the race is prefixed or the horses are drugged."

"What?" Pete exclaimed. "No, no my friend. Let me tell you the secret. It's all about the skills of the jockey. Just look at the favourite." They all got up to salute when the bell rang and the race began. Everyone screamed out their support for their favourites. Pete kept pointing at Ambrosino. Underneath the loud chanting, the loud vibration of a cell phone echoed. Danny waved to Pete. "It's mine. Just keep up with the game."

"Hello honey," he said.

"Hi. Juan and Nick have been asking if they could go to Wendy's house this afternoon."

"It's no problem. First check with Wendy if she is free today to have them around. I wouldn't want them to disturb her."

"Sure, will do. How is the race?"

"Sorry, honey. I can't hear you now. There is too much noise here. I will tell you about it when I get home. Bye."

Pete turned again to Danny and pointed to the race. "Look, Danny, Ambrosino is going at a consistent pace. He maintains his position in the first five. He is making sure none of the other jockeys gets past him. He is trying to preserve the horse's energy."

Danny quickly interrupted. "No way, Pete, you can't race a horse like an athlete, with the ability to strategise. I mean, you know, horses can't think for themselves."

"Come on Danny, look at him. He is doing the thinking for

the horse." Danny began shaking his head in disbelief as he watched Ambrosino, behaving exactly like Pete's description.

As usual the favourite won. Pete was shouting out and boasting to Danny, proud that his theory seemed to be founded. "You see, Danny, I am a pro in the game. I understand every element of it, even the behaviour of the horses. I guess I should be in that business." Danny kept on nodding his head but this time in confusion. "I still believe they dope the horses or in fact prefix the race. I love Ambrosino. But to keep on winning in such similar a fashion is a little dubious. I am sure something is not right."

"What Danny, so who are you now? Biblical Thomas? Well, you might as well bring in Carmen."

"Carmen? For what?" Danny exclaimed.

"To investigate your allegations, of course."

"Oh, yes. You really have a point there. Carmen will investigate anything from a runaway bride to missing pets. He is so strange. He acts daft like, like…"

"Colombo?" Pete chimed in.

"Yes. Like Colombo. Yet he still manages to solve any case, no matter how complicated it is."

"I completely agree with that," said Pete. "It's amazing. Anyway, it's been an interesting race. It's been fun."

Stuck in a long queue of traffic, the two race buddies talked happily in the car. Pete suggested that Danny return to his house to spend the rest of the day with him, but wondered if Lucy would need him to help with anything.

"Lucy would be working in the garden with Celeste and possibly having one of those 'love' chats," he said.

"Sure, yeah. Allow her to keep the poor old woman company. Well, I guess we turn the day into a race day," Pete laughed.

Wendy arrived earlier than expected to pick up Nick and Juanita. Lucy hurried to get the children packed and ready. She felt a bit scared and insecure about Wendy winning over her family, but assured herself that her personal friendship with Wendy and her utmost faith in Danny guaranteed a healthy relationship between Wendy and her family. She heard a faint voice calling out her name outside the house. She rushed out and saw Celeste standing over the hedge, already dressed for gardening. Celeste waved, and came forward. "Are you going to be gardening today?"

"Oh, yes, Celeste, I definitely will. Nick and Juan are visiting a friend so I will have enough time."

For both women, they always tried to utilise their free time on Saturdays to do what they loved around their homes. It was also a time when they met to talk about their life. Celeste, curious, stretched out her neck over the hedge to see the stranger. Lucy waved at Wendy as she walked towards her. Celeste gazed blankly at Wendy.

"Oh, Wendy. This is Celeste, my neighbour. Well, she is more like a mother to me. She keeps me company around here," Lucy smiled and strapped Juanita's backpack onto her daughter's back. Celeste extended a hand to Wendy.

"Are you the one taking my angels to your home?" she asked.

"Yes ma'am," said Wendy, politely trying to gain Celeste's trust. Juanita quickly ran to Celeste and waved at her, smiling. The old woman waved back and shouted to Nick, "How are you, my boy?"

"Fine, thank you," Nick responded, waving back at her.

Whilst walking to Wendy's car, Celeste called out to Wendy and said, "Please take good care of them for me, okay?"

Wendy could see and understand the old woman's concern. "Sure, ma'am, I definitely will," she said.

"Wow, I guess it's now time to do some gardening. I will get inside, change, get my tools from the garage and will be with you in few minutes," Lucy said, as she walked away to the house.

Time had passed since Celeste had last heard of Andy, and she was a bit concerned that her comments earlier had resulted in his absence. She quickly turned to Lucy and asked her about the possibility of Andy coming over to do some gardening. Lucy could sense the guilt in her voice, and assured her that there wasn't enough work to do in the garden to warrant his services at this time. "It's just us today," she said.

The two women performed their passionate duties with pride and contentment. Celeste stood over her colourful roses clipping, pruning the puny ones, and cutting fresh ones to place in a vase in her bedroom. Lucy knelt down by her rose plants, watering and loosening the soil around the base of each one to allow the water to filter through the rich loamy soil. They kept talking happily, laughing, but Celeste paused. She picked one big white rose, and lifted it towards Lucy.

"Do you know the story about roses?" she asked.

"No, not really," Lucy replied.

"Well, let me tell you. Roses bring out our inner expressions and feelings. It is not just the smell." She touched one of the petals. "You see this, how clean and pure it is. When a man gives you roses, he is trying to show you the kind of love he is offering."

"Really? Is it always like that?" Lucy asked, surprised.

"My dear," Celeste smiled, "it's supposed to be that way, but sometimes it's up to us women to test whether the inner expressions are true and sincere."

"Hmmm," Lucy smiled, nodding, showing her willingness to take some advice from the experienced old woman. "Lucy, your phone is ringing." Lucy excused herself and ran inside.

She came back to the garden, apologised to Celeste for leaving her alone for what she thought was a long time. Celeste smiled at her. "No worries. I've almost finished."

"It looks like your angels will not be coming home this night. They said they want to stay over at Wendy's house," said Lucy.

"Hmm. I guess that is not a bad idea. I think a change of environment is good for them." Celeste turned, released the knob of her front door, and lifted one of the roses to Lucy. "Did you know that Abraham gave me a bouquet of roses the night he proposed to me?" Curious, and musing over the new discovery about her beloved friend, Lucy stood there speechless. Celeste waved her hands at her. "Don't worry, I will tell you all about that another time."

Wendy sat by Juanita, trying to tuck her in. Nick, who was lying on the bed, was unusually quiet - at least for what Wendy had seen of him so far.

"Goodnight, sweet dreams." She turned and switched the inside light off, leaving the reflection of the outside light in the room. Closing the door, she heard Nick praying.

"Please God; help me to be like Christ, so I can feed five thousand people with the five dollars Daddy promised me."

Wendy, who was eavesdropping, stood there speechless, touched her heart and whispered, "Amazing!"

V

Danny sat behind his desk, intensely focused on the documents in front of him. He could tell he'd been extremely busy for the past few weeks, but he had never been so sure and fulfilled in his work up until now. He picked up his handset and called out to Wendy. He requested that she bring him the documents he'd asked her to retype and photocopy. Wendy quickly rushed into Danny's office with the files. She made sure one last time that she had everything in order. He always gave positive compliments about her accuracy and efficiency. Personally, she felt she was losing her sense of control and posture under the current workload. She realised from school that she was not particularly good at working under pressure. But given the freedom and time, she worked to perfection, sometimes beyond her own expectations. She ran back to her desk to check if she had left any of the documents behind. "It's alright, it's perfect," she sighed, heading towards the office.

She knocked, opened the door and handed over the files to Danny. He seemed unprepared to be distracted from what he was doing. He stretched his hands, taking the files from Wendy.

"Sir, they are all in the folder," she said, and realising talking was the last thing he'd want at that time, she smiled, apologised and left the office. Danny reached for the phone once again. He called Pete to discuss his work in progress. Pete answered with a little bit more concern, knowing their challenge. Danny relaxed for the first time in the day. "I just finished the tender and I will be sending it over to the Department of Housing – to Martin - this week," he said, assuring Pete he was really in control of the process.

"I see, but don't worry; when Martin sees my name on the documents, he wouldn't think twice about it. We will be just fine," said Pete, laughing with confidence.

"I know, Pete, but remember Carl and his views on giving out unmerited contracts. He has asked the president to sign a new policy on government contracts and I am not really sure of the details yet."

"You have a point. No matter what those policies are, we both know that we are good for it. Just look at how far we have come. We have the experience and the competence. We will be just fine," Pete said.

"Alright then. I need to tidy up one or two things at the office, so we will talk later."

"Good luck to us. See you then," Pete said.

Danny picked up the handset again and dialled Carl's number. In spite of his confidence and preparations, he was sure he needed the advice and opinion of the man the president even consulted before making important decisions. It wouldn't cost him anything, although Carl was highly paid by the government for his services.

"Hello Carl. It's me, Danny," he said.

"Hi Danny, how are you? Have you finished preparing your tender?" Carl asked.

"Yes, I have. In fact I will be submitting it by the end of this week," Danny laughed, trying to hide his nervousness.

"That's great. I wish you all the best."

"Thanks, Carl." He paused for a minute. "Can you tell me a little bit about the new government contract proposals?"

Carl sensed Danny's desperation, but politely declined. "No, Dan. I am sorry, I can't. But relax; the full report will be out before they announce the outcome of the bid. I promise to call you before then."

"I understand, Carl. Thanks anyway."

"It's okay. Dan, there is a government dinner at the government's guest house and I am inviting you and Pete," he laughed. "Courtesy of Carl Lennon. I guess I owe you that."

Danny touched his tie, and loosened it up.

"Really? Thanks, Carl. Pete will be excited. We will surely meet you there."

"Sure, but hey, bring the wives."

Danny got on the phone. He eagerly wanted to talk to Pete about the good news. He had always wanted to dine with his heroes, but never imagined it in this way. He was sure he would meet people who exuded courage and success, and though he was not threatened, he definitely knew he had to be well prepared to meet the men who inspired him so. The phone rang a little bit longer than usual; he suspected Pete might be busy with his work.

Pete had done well for himself by creating a consortium of international conglomerates with an excellent reputation. For him, life was more about pleasure than having to work all the time. "Life is too short," he would say. But though he would like to have fun, he always gave his maximum effort to his businesses. Pete sat in his home office reading his business deals, making sure to finish them so he could have the rest of the week off.

"Hello Danny. Any good news?" he asked, answering his cell phone.

"Yes, there is. I just spoke to Carl, and guess what? He invited us to the government's dinner this weekend. At the government's guest house!"

"Whoa! Hold it right there. Come on, Danny, quit messing with me. Is this one of your jokes?" Pete asked, suspiciously.

Danny kept on laughing. "No, I am not messing with you. This is real. I mean as real as Ambrosino." Pete was silent for a moment while he considered the offer. "You see, Dan, we are already rolling with the big guns. I bet you it's a sign of us winning the contract. We are almost there."

Danny quickly interrupted. "Come on, Pete, don't be too superstitious. We have the right to be happy, though."

"It's hardly superstition! I am telling you a fact."

"Well, whatever you say. I won't argue with you. Do tell Linz and I will let Lucy know. I am actually looking forward to it myself. It will be great."

"I'll tell her now. You know how Linz loves such occasions," said Pete.

Linz was open and free-spirited. Pete loved that about her. She would chat with all the important personalities and make a positive impression on them at ceremonial occasions. Pete sometimes felt a little bit insecure about having her around all those personalities, but his fears were always unjustified. She never showed any lustful interest in them, despite a few modest flirtations. "Sometimes a little harmless flirting opens up business opportunities," he would say.

Danny stood behind the wardrobe in his bedroom. He tried to hide the light red silk dress. He had bought it specially from Lucy's favourite designer, a dressmaker who specialised in custom-made dresses for important occasions. He was sure it would be as much of a surprise as the news of the invitation. To ensure it wasn't too obvious, he covered the dress with some of Lucy's old clothing. He smiled and began whistling, walking proudly into the kitchen. He inhaled deeply; taking in the smell of Lucy's cooking.

"Hi honey. How are you doing with the cooking? I missed you today. And this smell!" He pointedly looked towards the pots on the stove. Lucy dried her hands on her apron and turned to kiss him. "What's the smile for, honey?" She could sense something unusual in his demeanour.

"Honey, there is a present for you in the bedroom." Lucy rolled her eyes at him, anxious and in wonder. "I can smell something fishy going on. What is it?" Danny tilted his head back, thinking for a minute, and shook his head. "I am not telling you. Just go and find out for yourself."

Lucy turned to the pot on the stove, reduced the power,

stirred the sauce, and headed to the bedroom with Danny. He stood by the door, smiling with pride. He knew she was not a big fan of such functions, but he was sure she would be enamoured by the dress. He watched Lucy as she carefully went through her wardrobe. Lucy jumped, giggled gleefully and picked up the dress. She placed it on the bed, "Wow, honey, this is beautiful!" She lifted the tag on the dress and screamed. "What? Eagle Pinely! Thank you! Thank you! It's Incredible. What's the occasion?"

Danny moved away from the door, getting close to her, his eyebrows raised. He was sure he wouldn't have to say anything further to convince her to honour the invitation. Holding her hands, he looked into her eyes. "Before I tell you, I will give you a task, a puzzle, and you have to start putting the pieces together from Saturday." Lucy became very curious. "What's happening on Saturday?" She could barely stand on her feet. She knew Danny was a man of many surprises but this time she realised there was something more to it. She pulled him to her body, each of them looking deeply into the other's eyes. "I can tell it's a ball from the style of the dress, but where? And whose is it?" Danny pulled away from her slowly. "Okay, you have the idea now so I will tell you. Carl invited us to a dinner at the government's guesthouse. We will be going with Pete and Linz this Saturday." Lucy was lost for words, trying hard to absorb the surprise. She knew that she could now hide behind Linz's free spirited personality to enjoy the occasion. Her immediate impulse was to call Linz, but, before running to grab the phone, she turned, picked up the dress, and carefully placed it on a hanger.

Danny, now content, continued. "A word of caution, though. The puzzle may or may not be solvable." Lucy was hardly listening, walking quickly back to the phone. She stopped pressing the keypad on the handset, turned to Danny and asked, "Honey, what time are we coming back home on Saturday? I need to arrange for the babysitter to come over for the children."

"Hmm. About three or four in the morning. I am not too sure," said Danny. "You know these events; if a contentious political debate starts it could go on all night. I hope nothing like that happens, but, if it does, I am sure Pete would love to stay another night. Could the kids stay with Celeste?" he asked. Lucy looked at him with concern. "Oh no, honey, the old woman needs her rest. I will call Carrie. If I call her right now, I am sure she will be able to make it on Saturday."

"Carrie?" Danny said, trying to figure out who she was. "Yeah, Carrie. Mrs Pasty's daughter," said Lucy. She began pressing the keys on the handset, paused, and said, "Honey, if the sitter is going to stay overnight, why don't I call Wendy."

"Wendy?" Danny said, his face betraying his scepticism. He had enjoyed working with Wendy at the office, but was uncomfortable with including her in his private, domestic life.

"Yes, Wendy. She is the only one I can trust to stay the whole night with the children alone in the house. I mean, apart from Celeste."

"No, honey, I don't think it's such a good idea. And besides, she'll probably have other plans on Saturday night," he said, in what he hoped was a convincing tone.

"I know, but I could give it a try. Maybe…"

"Sure, sure, if you insist," he interrupted.

"Oh, Wendy. Thank you very much. You are a true friend. Good night," Lucy said on the phone. She turned to Danny. "It's sorted now. She will come over on Saturday. I will call Linz and talk to her about the occasion."

"Sure, sure," Danny said, walking out of the bedroom.

On Saturday night, Wendy sat on a chair in the children's bedroom reading a bedtime story to Juanita and Piper. She turned over to the last page and read, "So the prince said to his new bride, I love you Princess Lillo. And he kissed her. The end."

Piper yawned, turned over, and said, "I feel sleepy now."

Wendy bent over and tucked Piper and Juanita in to their beds. "Goodnight girls," she said, kissing their foreheads.

"Goodnight, Aunt Wendy," they replied.

Ruby was lying on her bed busily looking through her drawing book. She loved drawing and particularly admired her new artistic creations every night before she slept. This time, she had drawn a caricature of Wendy and was trying hard to make it real. Wendy moved over to her, picked up the drawing, and could admit it really did look like her.

"Wow, this is amazing, Ruby. That's me. Exactly like me," she encouraged. "May I keep it?"

Ruby nodded. "Yes, you can."

"Thank you. But, for now, you have to take a rest. It's very late. You can draw more tomorrow, okay? Goodnight."

"Goodnight," she replied.

"Nick, may I give you a kiss?" Wendy teased, standing at the door to Nick's room.

"No, thank you," Nick responded.

Wendy wished Nick had accepted the offer. She would have loved to get closer to the shy boy, to help him overcome his reticence with women. *No, it's okay for him to be that. He is just a kid*, she thought. She could remember Bobby, the little bashful boy in her class at primary school who later married three women – not legally, though – on his twenty-fourth birthday. *Nick will pick it up as he grows*, she thought.

"Don't worry, I understand," Wendy smiled. "Goodnight, Nick."

VI

Danny and Pete sat in Danny's office, wondering what news might emerge by the end of the week. Almost all the parties in the building construction industry had been keenly waiting for the outcome of the bid. For Danny and Pete, the outcome scared them far more than the challenges the project itself involved. They had invested a huge amount of time, energy, and money in the bid.

Danny sat on his chair with lax shoulders and sweaty hands. Pete moved towards him.

"Don't worry, Danny. We will get this contract, and know that if we get it you are set for life. I am ready to bet my whole life on it. You just focus on the work and I will worry about the financing. Anyway, with the government's new proposals on contract financing, we will be home and dry."

He could see Danny's face beaming with a little hope now. Danny was smiling and nodding with confidence. He looked at Pete and said, "Let's hope for the best. I've been told that there were a large number of competitive bidders and, as usual, Dennis was among them. You know as well as I do how he's tried to manipulate the government in the past. Thanks to Carl, he's not getting his way, but still, I cannot stop feeling scared of him. He is so corrupt and unpredictable."

"It doesn't matter, Danny. We still have to stay positive. Let's just relax and see what happens. Or should I say que sera sera," said Pete.

"Yes, you are right. I am somehow confident because I included the new supplier's quotation in the tender. Zelly supplies high quality materials at low prices. I guess I should believe in us and the system." Danny paused. "Yeah, I think I should."

"You are now talking like the Danny I know. By the way, when and how did you contact Zelly?"

"I began negotiations with them the very moment I heard that the government was going to announce this contract. I called their office and they were more than glad to work with us. Their products last a long time as well. An association with them will boost our reputation."

Pete could admit he was really impressed by Danny's efforts. He never doubted Danny's skills on the job, but this act indicated a man who understood and would do whatever it took to get the job done. "Damn, Danny, you are so good. Incredible, in fact."

"That's me," said Danny. "And…" He paused, having been interrupted by the sound of the office phone. He pushed his chair forward and reached for the handset.

"Sir, there is a Mr. Carl on the line," said Wendy.

"Okay, put him through immediately. Hold any calls in the next few minutes."

"Congratulations, Dan," said Carl.

"Finally…"

Danny interrupted, screaming. "Yes! Yes!"

Carl was convinced he'd gotten the message. He had tried several times to be allusive and obscure to surprise people but he'd realised that good news should be told as it is. He laughed. "You won the contract, although Dennis gave you a run for your money." Danny pressed the speakerphone button to allow Pete to hear what was going on. He could see he wanted to unravel the reason for his scream. Pete was good at maintaining his calm without explicitly showing his desperation to hear any news. Danny knew this was no ordinary news. It should come straight from the horse's mouth.

"The government will be announcing it today, but I just felt the need to let the cat out of the bag first."

Pete quickly deduced what had just happened, and commented, "Carl, do you know you have just changed the destiny of…"

Carl interrupted. "I know. Come on, Pete, I know you guys are destined for greatness. Danny was telling me last time about his retirement plans."

"Sure. It starts this minute."

Danny was pacing up and down in his large office. He stood still for a minute, moved to the phone and said, "Carl, we too are happy with the new proposals. Now we will get our certified invoice payments on time."

"Sure, yes. It will certainly remove any abuse or delay in the payment process. Anyway, I gotta go now. Good luck to you guys," Carl blessed them.

"Thanks, we won't forget you. You are the best!" Danny and Pete said, concurrently.

The smiles on their faces accurately displayed their emotional and professional satisfaction. They knew this would be their last job and the jackpot, for that matter. They both picked up their coats from the chair and headed off out of the office. Pete turned to Danny. "It's now time to tell the ladies. We can now tell them with pride and I dare say we'll definitely be getting some love tonight," he said with a wink.

"Definitely," Danny concurred.

Wendy kept talking on the phone. She saw Danny and Pete walking happily out of the office. She looked up at them, smiled but refused to be distracted, though she did wonder why they were in such high spirits. She waved to them and resumed her chat. Unbeknownst to Danny and Pete, she was chatting with Lucy. The two women had developed such a bond, talking several times a week on the phone and sharing their thoughts on life. Wendy expressed that she was looking forward to seeing Juanita and Nick, and, more importantly, to be in the arena of *feminine* discussions. Wendy seemed to have been enjoying more and more the company of the woman who spoke little of herself, but patiently listened to other people. *I am sure if I spoke to Lucy a lot, I could find out more about her*, she thought.

Lucy carefully arranged her cookware. She kept sorting out her ingredients for Wendy's visit on Saturday. Wendy always came for her visits immaculately dressed, so she was definitely also a fan of cleanliness. They both believed the old saying that 'cleanliness is next to Godliness'. Lucy sometimes would wonder if Wendy was a practitioner of it at home, but she was not fixated on that because their friendship was more important than personal judgements.

Danny tiptoed into the kitchen, and tickled her waist. "Honey, the eagle has landed." His face beamed with smiles.

"Looks like someone's had a lucky day," said Lucy, rolling her eyes at him.

"I certainly have. A lifetime blessing! Are you still putting together the pieces of the puzzle?" he asked.

"Let me guess. It's got to do with you being happy today, right?"

Danny began nodding gleefully, imploring Lucy to keep on guessing.

"You've had a new contract, that much I can tell. But what thing could have put you in this mood? I have already figured out that you might be bidding for a new contract. So…"

"Not just a new contract," Danny interrupted. "It is *the* contract. The one I discussed with you a year ago," Danny added. "No way!" Lucy looked up in the air. "Thank you, God." She rubbed her hands on the apron and embraced him, clinging on to his neck so hard that he could feel her excited heart fluttering in her bosom.

Danny absorbed the affection for some time, and then eased out of her grip slowly. "Honey, you can now have anything. I mean *anything* you want. Just name it and it's yours."

Lucy began shaking with surprise. She knew he'd always tried to give her everything she ever needed, but offering her the whole world? She looked deeply into his eyes, and said, "I know, honey, but I already have everything I would ever want: I have a loving husband and two wonderful children."

Danny was filled with pride. He loved her sincerity and above all how fulfilled being married to him made her. He smiled, and said, "That reminds me. I need to talk to the kids about it. They are part of this news." He kissed Lucy's forehead, raced into Juanita's bedroom, and called out, "Nick, can you come over here?"

Juanita sat on Danny's lap, with Nick sitting on a chair near them. Danny was rubbing his hands in Juanita's hair, making sure they understood how serious what he was about to ask them was. He patted Nick on the shoulder.

"Nick, if I were to tell you that you could ask me for anything and I would promise to get it for you – anything you wanted - what would you ask for?"

Nick's eyes began sparkling with excitement. "Anything, Dad?"

"Yes. Anything," Danny repeated.

Nick's face changed, showing more sadness and concern. He remained silent for a minute, and asked Danny. "Could I have another bike, Dad?"

Danny was a little bit surprised and confused. He turned to his son and said, "But Nick, the one you have is still new, the latest. You chose it yourself. Why don't you ask for something else?" he suggested. Nick had a way of conveying his feelings when dismayed, but Danny saw that, this time, he really felt passionately about his request. "Come on, Nick," Danny said, trying to placate him.

Nick looked down. "I know. There is this boy in my class, Jimmy, Who is always sad. And lonely. Nobody likes to play with him because they think he is too poor. So I was thinking, maybe I could give him a bike as a gift, just to make him happy," he said, now looking directly into Danny's eyes.

"Wow, Nick. That's good of you. But maybe he doesn't really need a bike to make him happy. You know what, why don't you bring him home one day after school, and we can ask him what he wants. I promise I will get him whatever he desires. If that's what will make you happy!" Danny could not believe his son's request initially, but he knew him too well to doubt Nick's good heart. Nick looked at his father with an appreciative smile. "Thanks Dad," he said, patting Danny's back.

Danny now turned to Juanita, making sure that she was not forgotten. She could not understand the emotions being expressed by Nick and Danny, but she knew they were definitely sharing something good. "So, Juan, what do you want?" he asked.

"Can I go to Celeste's house tomorrow for some cookies?" she asked innocently, showing her desire to see the old lady. She far preferred making cookies with Celeste than with her mother, mainly because Celeste always let her do the mixing. Danny smiled, brushing his hands through her hair. "Sure, you can, but what should Mom and I buy you as a present?" he asked. Juanita, thinking deeply, looked in the direction of her toys and pointed. "Can you buy me a newer, bigger Barbie? Please."

"Deal. It's done. You can have as many as you like," Danny promised. She couldn't hide her excitement, jumping off from his lap and onto her bed. "Thank you, Daddy. I love you."

Danny picked her up and kissed her forehead. "I love you, too."

Danny walked into his bedroom and found Lucy sitting on the bed leaning against a pillow. He leapt onto the bed, sat by her, and asked her a question. "Honey, do you know what I am thinking?"

"Not really. But tell me what's going on in that clever head of yours?" She rolled her eyes towards him. He moved close to her, perhaps an inch from her mouth. "I am going to buy a new house. In the countryside. A small ranch."

"What? You mean a place to race horses?" Lucy interrupted, trying not to sound incredulous.

"Absolutely not," Danny pleaded. "Honey, just a place to raise the horses and ride them personally. And, if there's time, *maybe* to race against Pete's," he laughed.

"I know exactly what to get you, my darling wife."

"Thanks, honey," said Lucy. "But really, I am content as I am." She kissed him, making sure he didn't push his offer further.

"Hmmm. Then why don't you let me taste the honey in this, huh?" He motioned to her body. They began kissing. Danny turned off the bedside lamp as they passionately enjoyed the pleasures of each other's bodies.

VII

Wendy had graced the Jeffney's house with her warm presence. This time, it wasn't a gathering but a division for common interest. The two women were happily chatting in the kitchen, reminiscing on the times they've shared during their friendship. Wendy wanted to know more about Lucy's personal life, but knew she should not push her luck. She had never seen Lucy sad or angry in the time that she'd known her. *I am sure she had a happy life as a child, and is having a happy married life now!* Wendy thought. She looked at Lucy and said, "They are really good kids. They really are."

"Nick and Juan?" Lucy asked, with raised eyebrows.

"Yes. They are amazing. How do you do it? I want to know," Wendy asked politely.

Lucy looked down, smiling with pride. She knew such a compliment - from a friend she had grown to trust - was definitely true and sincere. She didn't know where to start or what to say. Wendy realised her friend was struggling to know at which point to start, but she knew Lucy was going to tell her things that would amaze her. With Lucy she always learnt new things about life. She said, in a relaxed tone, "Do you know that the other night I heard Nick praying?"

"Oh, yes. I try to teach them to pray every night before they go to bed. You know, if you teach children the right way and the correct way to make choices, you can be sure that even without you telling them what to do, they will do the right thing."

"I see," said Wendy. "But I heard him praying that God should make him be like Christ so he could feed five thousand people with the five dollars Mr. Jeffney promised him. Well I stood there speechless. A selfless kid like that would certainly be one of the richest men in the country. It wouldn't surprise me at all."

Lucy was now laughing, looking straight into Wendy's eyes. For what more could a mother ask than to have such an incredible son! She really was doing a good job. "Well, at least then there wouldn't be any more starving people in the world," Lucy added. Both women looked into each other's eyes, smiling at the possibility of something good happening in the world. Lucy turned to Wendy. "My father was the head of a business consortium. He travelled all the time, which meant we hardly saw him at home. My mother, too, spent all her time in the courtroom, buried in cases, as a way to cope with the loneliness." For the first time, Wendy was beginning to feel Lucy's emotions.

"Hmmm. That must have been hard on you," she said.

Lucy smiled, taking Wendy by surprise. "No, not at all," she said. "In fact, we had quite a loving home. We were practically raised by my Aunt Doris. My sister and I used to call her 'the heart's resolve'. She was composed in any situation; it didn't matter how bad it was. One day, my sister came home crying. She refused to talk to anybody but my Aunt persuaded her to talk to her. My sister said the boys at school would not love her. And the male staff would not drool over her, no matter how seductively she acted. The men in the neighbourhood would not look at her twice. She wanted to know what was wrong with her. She felt like dying. My aunt looked deeply into her eyes and said to her 'a decent woman would not exchange her honour for her life. And if any man gives you a reason not to, just embrace it gracefully'."

Wendy stood there with her jaw dropped. "Wow, I can't believe it. And your sister?" she asked in wonder.

"Yes. My elder sister," Lucy replied. "Well, she doesn't visit me because she thinks I failed to fulfil our father's dream – he wanted us to run his company - by marrying Danny and moving here with him," Lucy paused, smiled and shrugged. "But I promised myself that I would do all I could to raise my children and never leave them alone by themselves. It wouldn't matter to me if their choices turn out to be different from what I expect of them." Wendy had managed to compose herself now. "That's sweet," she said, looking outside at the lucky man playing with his children.

Celeste came out of the hedges in the garden with a jar of cookies in her hands. She was trying to keep the jar steady in her frail hands, calling out to the children in the garden. "Hi there."

Danny turned to her, brushing the grass from his shorts. "Hello, Celeste. How are you doing today?" he asked.

"I am alive and well. Much better than yesterday," she said.

Danny had been busy for a while, so had not spoken much with Celeste lately. Previously, he had helped Celeste with her house repairs whenever he had some free time. "It's good to hear you are well," Danny said. Juanita and Nick ran to Celeste. Juanita quickly wrapped her arms around the old woman, asking, "Are these cookies?" She pointed to the jar.

"Sure, angel. I made them for you and the family." She handed the jar to the girl. Juanita's smile showed her deep appreciation. "Thank you, Celeste."

Nick, moving closer, waved and said, "Thank you, Celeste."

"Come on, you know you are always welcome," she said. Danny moved towards Celeste, touching her shoulder. "You look younger and younger each day, Celeste," he said. "Would you mind me taking you out on a date sometime?" He winked at her, causing Celeste to blush. "Hey, you silly boy. Wait till I tell the lady of the house." They both burst out laughing and Celeste watched as Danny resumed the game with the children.

Lucy cleared her throat, looking away, and continued. "Danny and Pete were best friends and roommates at university. Linz was my roommate and had just started dating Pete. One day, just after our graduation ceremony, there was a party on Danny's campus and Linz convinced me to go with her." She paused and laughed. "I was the shy one, a little bit scared, but Linz always could make anybody do anything she wanted. At the party, almost everyone was dancing, and Danny and Pete were at the centre of the crowd. They were dancing carelessly, and a bit drunk." Wendy exhaled, trying to imagine her boss dancing brazenly.

"Linz," Lucy continued, "went over to convince Danny to come and chat with me at the table. As he walked towards me my heart began pounding, my mind went blank."

"Were you scared or just confused?" Wendy asked.

"Oh, everything," said Lucy. "So, as he got close to the table, he slipped and I leaned forward to assist him, but he fell right into my arms. And we were staring straight into each other's eyes. Then the crowd began shouting, thinking that he wanted to kiss me. 'Kiss! Kiss! Kiss!', they were chanting. My whole body shut down. I couldn't move any of my muscles, but he pressed his body firmly against mine and kissed me," Lucy smiled, touching her hair as she did so.

"Wow," said Wendy, rolling her eyes and touching her heart.

"Yeah, I know. That was my first kiss and the following year, on the very same day, he proposed to me," said Lucy. Wendy looked outside again, this time staring at Danny differently having learned of his romantic tendencies. She now realised why he'd always walk into his office with a smile on his face. Lucy saw Wendy looking at Danny with a different stare, but she understood any woman would look at Danny that way after discovering his charming personality.

"So, enough about me. How about you? Is there a special someone?" Lucy asked, causing Wendy to snap out of her thoughts.

"Me? No. Not yet, anyway. I guess I am waiting for him to fall right into my arms," Wendy said.

"Well then, don't give up. I am sure he will someday. Maybe at the celebration dinner here." Wendy smiled. "I might take my chances though. In fact, I definitely would."

VIII

Danny paced the floor of his large office, desperately trying to figure out what was happening to him. He was confused about whether or not he wished that that night could have gone on forever. Thoughts of Wendy occupied his mind the whole of the night through, and he found himself imagining things he never had before. Carmen's voice on the dinner night echoed in his ears. "Come on Dan, how can you lick this fine bone without having a bite at it?" He stood alone in his office, knowing that if he was smart about it, he could definitely execute his lewdest desires. He practiced for the final time the words he was going to use to achieve them. He was certain he was going to have it easy. He exhaled deeply, rubbing his palms against each other and blowing through the small gap between them. Somewhat collected, he pulled his chair out from underneath the desk and sat down, ready to advance. Wendy knocked on the door and entered.

"Sir, I have the report and…" She froze at the lusty look in Danny's eyes.

"Hey, Wendy, how are you today?" he asked, his eyes fixed on her cleavage. He pushed his chair back, got up and moved towards Wendy.

"I'm okay, I guess," she replied, her voice shaking a little. She tried to avoid looking straight at him; Danny's eyes could seduce even the coldest woman. Wendy looked away, still with an outstretched hand trying to give Danny the file.

Danny was now eye-to-eye with Wendy. He could see her shivering, and she seemed to have lost control of herself. Danny was sure he was in control, but had little time to consider whether he was delusional or if his advances scared Wendy. "Good, because I am in particularly rude health today," he said, raising his eyebrows, and nodding. "In fact, I am on fire."

"So I see, sir. This contract is really having such an impact on you. I am happy about it, too," Wendy said.

"It sure is having an impact on me! But not as much as you are now." Danny moved his eyes over Wendy's body. He noticed that Wendy had upgraded her appearance to reflect the company's new standing. Still perplexed, she turned and, for the first time, looked directly into his eyes.

"Sir, are you okay?" she said, trying to figure out what was happening to her boss.

"Sure, sure," Danny said, taking Wendy's hands in his, fingering her manicured nails.

Wendy recoiled. She was scared she might appear disrespectful.

"Please, sir, I don't think…"

"*Don't* think at all," Danny interrupted. "The only thought you have to concern yourself with now is me. I have not been appreciating such a beauty, and it bothers me. I should have been…"

"No sir, but…" Wendy interrupted.

"It wasn't only Carmen who noticed you last night. Trust me, I really do care," said Danny, still gazing at her cleavage.

"Please sir, I don't mean to be rude, but be careful with words. *Care* is a scary word when you're as scarred as I am," Wendy interrupted, looking away again.

"Wow. I never knew you were a poet," he teased. "That's good, but…" He paused, pulling her into his arms. *He is a strong man.* Wendy thought. *Maybe talking him out of his intentions would be a better option.* She wanted to resist by pulling away, but the charm in his eyes coupled with his touch was irresistible. She stared, breathless in his arms.

"But what about your wife? I can't do this."

"Do what? She will not know; that is, if you don't tell. Look, I promise you…"

"Sir, don't," Wendy interrupted. "Don't make promises you can't keep," Wendy pleaded, still in his arms. "I guess it would work on a woman who loves…"

"Shhh." Danny put his finger on her lips. "I know she loves me. But just, just…" He moved his lips towards her lips. Wendy stood there helplessly panting for breath. The contours of his mouth touched her smooth luscious lips. The phone, which had been ringing for some time by this point, remained unanswered.

"Please sir, pick that up, or at least let me," she begged.

Danny finally released her from his grip and reached for the phone. "Hello. Jeffney speaking."

"Hey pal, what's up?" Pete's voice echoed through the phone.

"Great, pal. Great," said Danny, turning to glance at Wendy as she smoothed her blouse and returned to her desk.

"Are you kinda in the middle of something?" Pete asked, recognising Danny's distracted tone.

"No. No. It's just that I've got some things to finish up. You know I'm never too busy for you," Danny replied, trying to make sure his guilt wasn't too obvious to Pete.

"Well I won't distract you a moment longer, I was just checking in. I'll see you at the race, I guess. Take care," Pete said.

"Sure. That's great," said Danny. "You know what; I will call by your place on the way home. There's something important I need to discuss with you."

"I will expect you then, then. Bye."

Danny picked up his coat, scrambled to his feet, rejoicing that he'd at least begun something promising. He rushed out of his office wearing a contented smile. He got to Wendy's desk, stopped and pointed his finger at her. "Think about it," he said. Wendy looked up at him. "About what, sir?" she asked, innocently. Danny laughed and flung his coat over his shoulder. "About the possibility."

Pete sat on the sofa with a glass of champagne in his hand. He wondered what it could be that was so important to Danny besides the impending project.

"So pal, how is life?" he asked.

"Couldn't be any better. How about you and the family?"

Pete could sense something in Danny's enthusiasm, in his body language too perhaps, but he tried not to read too much into it. He knew Danny too well to make any assumptions. "They just left for shopping," he said. Danny composed himself and sat down comfortably. He crossed his legs and cleared his throat. He was ready to spill on his conquest.

"What's up with you? Are you okay?" Pete asked, seeing Danny fidgeting in the chair.

"Yeah, I am. It's just that there's something I've got to tell you." He paused, thinking it over for a second.

"What is it that you are hiding? Just spit it out. I am all ears," Pete encouraged, trying to make him feel at ease.

"Nothing. But there is something strange happening to me. I mean, it's really strange. I cannot explain it though. Did you see Wendy at the party?" Danny asked, turning away from Pete.

"Sure. There were lots of people and I must have met almost half of them."

"No," Danny insisted. "I mean. I kind of… I have been thinking about her since then. I am beginning to…" Pete interrupted him. "I hope I'm not thinking what you are thinking. And if you are thinking what I'm thinking now, then forget it. I mean forget about it instantly. I don't want to be part of it. Count me out.".

"Come on, you of all people can't deny she has the…"

"The what? Don't be silly. What in the world would make you even conceive of such an idea in the first place? Are you out of your mind?"

Danny looked down in embarrassment but was determined not to let the point drop. He knew he had to make his feelings known. "Today I held her in my arms and…"

"You what? That far? What do you think Lucy is going to do

when she finds out? Why do you want to risk everything you hold dear in your life?" Pete kept on interrogating him. He wasn't expecting instant answers, but he knew he had to beat the devil out of his beloved brother before he ruined his life. He was Danny's last hope of redemption.

"Yeah," Danny said, in discomfiture. "She will not find out. It's not as if it happened at home."

"At your office? Please have some decency. Lucy and Wendy are like sisters now. I don't even want to imagine it. And I am sure you wouldn't like to imagine it either," said Pete, turning away in disgust. Danny realised he was fighting a losing battle. If he was to find validation for what he so desired to do, he needed to be more convincing. He was not ready to back down, despite Pete's insistence.

"This is no big crime, you know. It's just a man having a little fun," he said.

"What? You call this a little fun. What kind of fun will you get from Wendy that you can't get at home?" Pete argued impatiently. Danny had no answer for this.

"It's just a few exercises before the real game."

Pete stared in shock. He was seeing a whole new side of Danny.

"What has come over you? Listen to yourself, you sound like a fool. I cannot believe what I am hearing. Do you believe what you are saying? I mean…" He was lost for words.

"Don't worry about me, Pete, I will be just fine."

Pete contemplated all that he had heard for a moment and then rose to his feet.

"Why don't you go home, eh? You are delusional. You need some rest."

Wendy sat, in tears, between her neighbours, Ruth and Orpah. She looked hopeless and helpless as she kept on sniffling. She knew she could find solace in her two friends. They had helped her get over her boyfriend when he dumped her a year previously. The two sisters urged her to divulge what was eating her up. "There is no problem without a solution," Ruth said, convincingly. She kept beating herself up. *Perhaps, I excessively adorned myself in the office*, she thought. She blew her nose on the tissue in her hand and moved forward on the sofa, looking at the anxious faces around her.

"He actually came on to me today. I don't know what's gotten into him. At first I thought he was happy, you know because of this big contract going through, but then he kept on and on, as if it was the first time he'd seen me," she said.

"What? Who? Your boss?" Ruth and Orpah asked.

Wendy began nodding. "Yes."

"Wow, that's amazing," said Orpah, relaxing, and throwing herself back onto the sofa.

"Shut up Orpah," Ruth rebuked.

"What? Isn't it romantic? I mean, this guy just landed the biggest project in the region and he's all the money: what do you think he is going to do with it?" Wendy tried to consider the possibilities. She was beginning to discover something she had not thought of before. Ruth quickly rebuked Orpah. "Don't you have any decency? This guy has a wonderful wife and amazing kids. Juan is an angel. Do you expect Wendy to break up such a loving family? Doesn't it bother your conscience?"

"Yes, it is true," Wendy chimed in. "I have developed such a deep love for the family. The kids, I am like a hero to them. Lucy is like a sister to me now. I cannot exchange this trust and love for money. Money is not everything you know, Orpah!"

Orpah shrugged. "Well, it's up to you. You have been waiting all your life for an opportunity to find money to set up your own business, and now you get this perfect opportunity and you want to turn it down. I guess you don't want to achieve your dreams. Anyway, he has achieved his and he wants to help you achieve yours."

"By cheating on his wife? Not a chance," said Ruth. "Wendy, don't listen to Orpah. She is just a fool and selfish. If you have to succeed, you must do so the right way; otherwise your conscience will never let you rest. As the good old book says, '...better to eat dry crust of bread where there is love, than to eat the finest meat where there is hate'," Ruth eulogised.

"You are right, Ruth. I really don't want to hurt anybody," Wendy paused. "But..."

"Yes. A part of you wants to do it, doesn't it?" Orpah asked. "Just go with your gut, not your heart or your head," she added.

"Orpah! Are you really that ruthless? I can't stand this anymore." Ruth got up and raced into the kitchen to make herself a cup of herbal tea; she needed something to calm herself down.

Orpah took advantage of Ruth's absence to reiterate her theory. "You see, my dear, this is just a fling. His wife will never know. And after you get what you want, you can just abandon him. Besides you'll have so much money, you'll never have to work for anyone again."

Sitting there, more confused than ever, Wendy wondered if she could consider Orpah's suggestion. She had been dreaming of setting up her own business, of being independent, of being in control of her life. Could this be the opportunity she had been looking for?

Orpah realised she was making progress. She rubbed Wendy's back reassuringly and moved closer to her.

"Think about your life, not someone else's happiness. Life is all about making it, and that is when money comes in. Go on. Just go for it."

Ruth, overhearing Orpah's last statement, raced to Wendy's side. "Wendy, I know this is confusing for you. But if I were you, I would rather listen to myself than to listen to this selfish soul," Ruth said, pointing at Orpah. Wendy buried her head in her hands and began sobbing. She kept shaking her head, "I don't know, I don't know what is right or wrong anymore."

IX

As she entered Danny's study, Lucy saw an unfamiliar file on the desk. Initially, she ignored it, wanting to re-arrange the ones scattered on the shelf first, but her curiosity drove her to the desk. She picked up the file and started perusing the contents.

"What?" she exclaimed. Danny had left behind the documents that required his final signature for the new contract. She quickly reached for the phone and called Danny's office. There was no response.

Lucy thought this was strange; Wendy never missed her calls. She tried Danny's cell phone: there was no response there, either. *Oh, maybe they are in a meeting together*, she thought. Taking the files with her outside the study, she hurriedly got the key to her new Chevrolet. *This will certainly spice up our love*, she thought, smiling to herself.

The drive to the office had taken less time than usual. She was surprised to see that the busy street that connected Danny's office to the highway was deserted.

On entering the reception, she noticed that Wendy was not at her desk. She continued into Danny's office, fantasising about the romantic appreciation she would receive for delivering the documents personally. She opened the door and saw Danny's suit on his desk. And Wendy's on the chair. She blinked twice, unsure of what she was seeing. Stretching her head, she saw Wendy's head a few inches from the table. The desk obstructed her view of Danny in the most compromising of positions.

"What?" she exclaimed, trying hard not to scream with rage.

The files fell from her hands. She turned and ran away from the office. She became numb, disorientated and began sobbing.

Wendy heard Lucy's voice and pushed Danny off her, pointing to the door.

"It's Lucy, your wife," she said, panting for breath.

"What?" Danny enquired, in disbelief. "How and when did she get here?" He looked at the door and found his documents on the floor. He ran after Lucy.

"I don't think she could understand anything you were to say to her now," said Wendy, pulling Danny back.

"Will you shut up? Do you know what you've caused? I... I... God! What is this?" Danny asked, rushing to the window to check if Lucy's car was still in the car park. It wasn't. He pushed Wendy aside angrily.

"Pete, Pete," he called out, his voice vibrating with fear and worry.

"Are you alright?" Pete asked.

"No. I am not, and it will get worse," said Danny.

"What do you mean? Please calm down and talk to me," Pete demanded, in a concerned tone.

"I need to see you. To talk to you. It's a matter of life and death. I mean it, I need to see you as soon as possible," Danny pleaded, sniffing, almost in tears.

"Okay, come to my house and..."

"No. Linz can't know," Danny interrupted.

"Alright. Meet me in the park near the community library. I guess it will be more private there," Pete said, doing his best to calm Danny.

"See you there," Danny said, slamming the phone down and heading straight for the door.

Lucy was completely out of touch with reality. Several thoughts ran through her mind. "How? Why? Is this the end of my life? Are fifteen years of marriage about to crumble because of a few minutes of passion? God, what is happening to me? To us? And Wendy? How could she?" She kept on asking herself questions.

She stopped at a traffic light when it indicated red. Many questions kept on swimming through her mind. She didn't notice when the light turned green and many cars piled up behind her blasting their horns at her.

A chauvinistic, selfish fat guy, who was parked behind Lucy, began hailing curses at her. A loud sound from a big trailer driving by the other side of the road echoed through Lucy's ears. She snapped out of her confused state. Quivering, she drove off. She couldn't focus.

"How can I allow her to be around the children again? Oh God! What will I tell Juan and Nick? Danny is their idol. He's their hero! Whom can I trust now? I could talk to Linz, I trust her; she's so blunt and straightforward. She will just tell me to go for a divorce. Would I divorce him? No. Not on my life. I love him so dearly." She wiped the trail of tears away but kept on sniffling. "And what about telling Celeste? She holds Danny in such high esteem."

She reached a tram crossing. The light turned red, the barrier started its descent. She sped on. In a blink of an eye, the tram came rushing in front of her. The people on the street began screaming, covering their mouths in fear, some closing their eyes to such oblivion. Then, as if someone had screamed her name in her head, she immediately regained consciousness and stepped on the brake as hard as she could. The car stopped just a few inches short of the tram's path. She began shaking again.

"Thank you God," she said, crossing herself. She turned and looked at the startled crowd that had gathered along the road.

"Is this worth my life?" she asked herself. "What will happen to Juan and Nick if I die? Oh, if Aunt Doris was alive, she would tell me what to do." She remembered that Aunt Doris gave her some motivational tapes before she died. Lucy knew she had kept a few in the glove compartment since the day she had acquired the car. She drove quickly to a park and began searching for the tapes. "Yes," she said, having found one.

Pete sat close to Danny on the reserved bench in the park.

"I warned you, Danny. I said that if…"

"Yeah. I know. But you are not to assign blame here. Please just help me get out of this mess." He paused. "I just know she is very angry and frustrated, she's probably at home contemplating a divorce," said Danny.

"Divorce?" Pete said, a little bit surprised. "For what? I don't think Lucy will want that, not even for the money. You and I both know that she does not need the money. Look at all that she left behind just to be with you."

"I know, but women are very unpredictable in situations like this. They will and can do anything," said Danny, smashing his hands on the bench, kicking through the air. He reached into his pocket, for a handkerchief and wiped away a trail of tears.

"Look. You and I have known Lucy for such a long time and she always looks composed and confident. Remember how she handled her Aunt's death?" Danny began smiling, sensing a glimpse of hope. He was nodding at the memory of that. Pete continued. "I know everything will be alright. Just go home. Pull yourself together, go home and talk to her. If you want, I can go with…"

"No, Pete," Danny interrupted. "I wouldn't want you to face the anger of a scorned woman." Pete kept shaking his head in disagreement.

"I really sometimes don't understand how life works, especially with women. They will run to you when you are a mystery, but will flee from you when you become a misery," Danny said, with a snort.

"I don't know, Danny. I guess you have to take them as they come. Maybe you get what you see, but trust me, with Lucy, I am sure you will always get more than that," said Pete.

"I don't get it. And I am not sure if I can understand," Danny said, burying his head in his hands. "God, I love her."

Pete got up from the chair and patted Danny on his shoulder. "Don't worry, Danny. You will understand someday."

Lucy leaned back in her seat, patiently listening to the voice on the tape. Reverend Johnson's voice came out of the speakers. He was reading from the good old book.

"*And now, I will show you the most excellent way. Love is patient, love is kind. It does not envy, it does not boast, it is not proud. It is not rude, it is not self-seeking, it is not easily angered, and it keeps no record of wrongs. Love always protects, always trusts, always hopes and always preserves.*"

She took in a deep breath and sighed. She looked up in the sky and said, "Thank you, God. Thank you, Aunt Doris. I am glad you left me this tape."

Lucy waited patiently for Nick and Juanita to come to the car. After a few minutes, the school bell rang and they came running out of the gate. With a smile on her face, she said to them. "Hello Nick, hi Juan."

"Hi, Mom," they responded.

"Mom, is Daddy home yet?" Juanita asked.

Lucy turned to her.

"No, not yet. But he will be home later."

Danny's car pulled into the driveway. He was discreet as he turned off his engine. Lucy ran to the garage to meet him, smiling as she did so. Danny stared at her for a minute and smiled, guilt visibly written on his face. Lucy wrapped her arms around him and led him into the house. She walked into the children's bedroom, reminding them to perform their nightly prayers and wished them good night. She then headed to her bedroom. Danny was sat on the bed, his back to the pillow, with an expectant look on his face. He knew he was in for it, and he was definitely expecting it to come. Lucy leaned forward, kissed him and lay beside him insouciantly.

Startled, he sat there for a few minutes staring at Lucy. He could not overcome his confusion anymore. He suddenly exploded. "Lucy, why are you tormenting me in this way? Why are you so calm, relaxed and comfortable and behaving as if everything is alright?" Lucy slowly sat up on the bed. The look in her eyes radiated sincere and true love. She placed her hands on his chest, caressing it gently. "Who am I to condemn you? Who am I to instruct you? No matter what happened today, you still came back home to me. You are still mine and I am still yours. Why fight for something that is already mine?" Tears rolled down Danny's face. "From now on, do with me as you please," he said, pleading with her. Lucy kissed him and slid under the sheets, full of smiles.

What Pete had said at the park began resounding in Danny's ears. He stared at Lucy, nodding, as he slid under the sheets, smiling as he turned off the bedside lamp.

My greatest fear is not doing right. And if I always do wrong, then I cannot run from my fears.

THE CHASING SELF

It's Christmas once again and I have to be ready for the family gathering. I can't always help it when Uncle Leo drinks himself into a stupor and vomits all over my room. Patty and her boyfriend make me feel uncomfortable, always displaying publicly what's meant to be secretive and beautiful. In a bid to spite me, Kenny, my older brother, always brags about his shrewdness and success. I know a time like this is supposed to bring joy and comfort but, for me, it's hell.

My name is Nibuem. I am a junior accountant. This is my story.

I wake up every morning at 5:00am to get to the office before all my colleagues. I start my work as normal; I am a normal guy, I guess. My colleagues have always had it in for me because I am dedicated to my work. The office is practically my home. After all, I only have to go home to Kitty - my cat - and sit alone behind the big screen in my living room. Work always was the only place I found any meaning in my life. I am good at what I do. I started as an assistant clerk and worked my way up to junior accountant. During that early time, I would dream of upgrading my life. I still go to the end of year party, but when it's over I go home still tied to my low position. To be honest, I don't blame them for not promoting me.

When we were children my father spent all his money on Kenny because he was the brightest. He and my Mom would talk all the time about how he was bound for greatness. I, on the other hand, always struggled at school. My father did not want to hear of me trying to apply to a college, but at least I had found something I was good at. The world of finance was my temple of solace, a place where I could define myself.

At the office party, Greg sat down beside a table that was surrounded by all the nice girls. I could tell just from looking at them that they had all the fun. Many empty bottles of beer were scattered on the table while the girls danced.

Douglas walked up to me, smiled, and for the first time made me an offer that until this day I still haven't understood. I was always the only guy in and out of the numerous parties all alone. I smiled back, stood up from my chair and walked uncomfortably towards a table of eight. Each guy had a lady with him, who was either kissing him or smiling happily. Douglas indicated for me to sit down by this blonde lady, who was happily watching the frolics of the others.

I introduced myself to her. "Hello, I am Nibuem."

"Hello, I'm Nancy," she said. Within minutes, I began sweating in my underarms. They all looked at me and offered me drinks. "Come on man, drink as many as you like. It's on the company," they said. As I took the bottle, I saw the face of Uncle Leo in one of his stupors, visibly on the bottle. I carefully put the bottle down, trying hard not to judge them. "I will have it later," I said. Nancy drew closer to me and began rubbing my shoulders. She started saying some things that I could barely understand. I panicked. I could see Patty and her boyfriend giving a public sexual display and I instantly felt sick.

"Sorry, Nancy, I need to use the bathroom."

I pulled away and left for the bathroom. I stood in the bathroom pondering the new direction my life had taken. "I have to leave this place," I said to myself. *This is not me. I need to be me.*

Walking down the busy road, I saw women offering their bodies, and men carelessly sucking and blowing cigarette smoke into the air. *Do they, by day, also have a square job like mine? Do they find happiness here or in their jobs?* I kept asking myself. Rounding the corner of my apartment building, I tried not to answer these questions myself because I was too scared of what I might find.

The following week, my day was going as it always did. Some of my colleagues looked busy behind their computers, while a group of them had gathered around Greg's desk and were laughing and giggling at something on his screen. As I was just about reaching my corner, Nancy waved at me. She was a new member of staff, it seemed. I smiled back and quickly sat behind my desk. Fully consumed in my work, I kept hitting the keys on the keyboard incessantly, as it gave me pleasure to do so. I only realised the time when everyone began leaving the office. I stayed in the office the whole night trying to find something to do. It was the best way to escape all the troubles and worries of life.

The following Saturday, I chose not to go to the office as early as I usually did. I spent lots of time in the bathroom because I could feel the drops of water soothing my skin. I stood in the bathroom wondering what exactly I would have to do at the office. Then, I looked up and saw an image in the old rusted mirror. Staring at me was a long bearded man with large eyeballs that penetrated faintly through the dense hair covering his face. Turning in fear, I yelled at the top of my voice. *Who is that stranger in my house?* I fled the bathroom with a sprint that would have won me an Olympic medal in the 100 metres. I kept running down the street until I saw an old woman sitting in front of her house. She looked at me curiously and asked, "Young man, why are you running?"

"There is a madman in my house," I replied.

"Really, are you sure?"

I became a bit agitated at her foolish questions, and I said, "Yeah, I'm sure. Why?"

Her gaze dropped to the lower part of my body. "Because I have just seen him running in front of me naked." That was the turning point of my life.

Early the next morning, I rushed to the hair salon and cut my hair. I shaved my beard and tried helplessly to organise my affairs. I wished I could do that with Kitty, but she had run away from the house – I wasn't giving her enough affection, I guess.

That night, I walked straight to a bar and sat down. A woman with curly brown hair walked up to me and said, "Hello, I am Julie. Can you buy me a drink?"

The old me would have said no.

"Of course I can."

I led her to the bar. She sat there listening to me as I kept on talking and talking about my life of solitude. She leaned towards me, kissed my cheek and said, "It's okay. Everyone has to choose a path in life, and I am sure you chose the one you did for a reason." The sense of meaning and happiness I felt was too much; it took my breath away. *Wow, at last, someone who understands me.* We left the bar and headed to my house. As we sat on the sofa, my whole body began to sweat. My hands were quivering as I lowered my left hand inside her blouse and began caressing her soft, luscious bosom. She smiled, looked at me, and patiently held my hand.

"No, Nibuem. Let's not make things complicated for now, eh? I think we should take it slowly." She briefly scanned the room and rose on her feet. "I can tell this place needs the touch of a woman," she said, teasingly. "Just relax and let me do the stuff I am good at." I stared at her as she cleaned and arranged the whole apartment. We later sat and chatted the whole night away. God, how I wished at the time that that night would never end.

I walked along the office corridor, whispering and manoeuvring my body to a tune in my head. My behaviour drew the attention of everyone in the office. "Hi, everybody!" For the first time, I had the confidence to wave to all of them.

I kept humming as I plunged into my office chair. I could hear someone calling my name. "Nibuem, come to my office now." The smile on my face disappeared instantly. *Oh, no. Am I going to be laid off? Please not now; not now that my life is moving on a new path.*

My boss kept smiling as I sat before him trying to figure out what was going to happen.

"Congratulations, Mr. Nibuem, you have just been promoted to Regional Finance Manager. The head office rang this morning and said they have seen your reports. In fact, when the job vacancy was announced, the board suggested I promote from within and so I picked you," he said. The chorus of praise in my heart resounded in my voice.

"Thank you. Thank you, sir. I don't know what to say. How can I thank…"

"No, Nibuem, don't thank me: you deserve it. You are one of the best employees this company has ever had."

When I got home that night, Kitty had returned and was lying on the sofa waiting for me. I looked at her in surprise. *What does she know?* As silly as it sounded, I still wanted to find out. I picked her up and we sat on the sofa to enjoy one of our favourite movies.

Next Christmas, I will be the first to get to the house. I will surprise them with the new me. I will smile, and before everybody leaves, I will give them the happy news; I will tell them that Julie and I are getting married.

When anything means nothing to us, everything will hardly mean something to us.

ANYTHING OR NOTHING

The busy, muddy street was full of people in a state of ecstatic celebration. It was time again for the annual festival in appreciation of good harvest. The event had attracted other small villages nearby because the people of Santano – a small African village - had enough to give some of their produce to them. The women, dressed in their traditional apparel and nicely woven straw skirts, danced around in rhythm with the drums. Behind the big tall drum was Kadaka, the town's biggest and strongest man, who always won the attraction of the young women with his unique skills. The women carried vats of cooked foods on their heads as they distributed them to spectators along the way. It was a distinguished procession as befit such a blessing.

In the corner of a hut sat Nkota, a poor hunter for whom times like these were a nightmare rather than a blessing. The presence of the high number of people in the village for the festival seemed to have a negative impact on the animals in the forest. For some weeks after the festival, no animal could be seen in the forest. He dozed off in front of his hut as the whole community turned into 'an exploding volcano' with shouts and laughter.

"When will these people stop all this fussing about and allow the animals to stay home?" he chuckled. If only he had a voice, he would definitely do something about it.

All he had was one childhood friend, Atonga, with whom he shared all his life and work. Together, they were the perfect team. Nkota, a master of custom-made rifles while Atonga, the brain behind traps that could catch the most cunning and strongest forest animal. Atonga could never resist having a dance at the procession in order to win the attention of Lobo, the most attractive young maiden in the village.

"Festival time is the only time of the year I feel completely lonely," Nkota said, ruefully chuckling to himself.

As they set off to the forest for their usual hunting journey, Nkota asked his friend, "Atonga are you sure you brought everything? I am not prepared to walk all the way home just because of your incompetence," he teased. They laughed because, of all the days, today was the day they were going to try the new custom-made traps.

"These will catch any animal that comes near them, I am positively sure," Atonga said. They found perfect spots where they set up as many traps as they could.

"Alright, now let's go home and wait until tomorrow," said Atonga.

"Yeah, I can't wait," Nkota replied.

Atonga sat under a tree with his shirt nicely folded on his lap to allow Lobo to notice his hairy chest. He hoped that the night would never end. After all the years, it had finally paid off to attend the annual procession. Lobo sat by him rubbing her smooth hands on his hairy chest.

"Wow, I am happy for you Atonga. I am sure with your new traps you are definitely going to catch as many animals as you can. I will have lots to cook," Lobo said.

"Oh, yeah, I can't wait to taste that delicious soup. The one you normally prepare for your father," said Atonga.

Lobo sat there for a few minutes, her happy expression changing to a dull one. "What's wrong, Lobo?" Atonga asked.

"Nothing really, nothing."

"Just say anything, I mean anything and it's yours," Atonga urged her.

"Well, if you put it that way. I know you are the one who designed all the traps, right?"

"Yeah, I did," Atonga said with confidence, as if to show his prowess to Lobo.

"Then why share the animals you catch with Nkota?"

"Don't go there! Nkota and I perfectly understand each other, and besides we have been friends since childhood. Sometimes he shoots prey and we share that equally too. It's perfectly okay with us."

Lobo pulled away from him. "If you want me to cook your favourite, then I need to have enough to give some to my family."

"Come on, Lobo. You will still have enough."

"Just this once. Nkota can shoot some animals for himself," Lobo retorted. Atonga sat down silently as if to consider the thought. "Yeah, you make a point, but remember just this time, okay?" he said.

"Good. This gesture shows me that you love me."

Atonga laughed contentedly and looked into the eyes of his new love.

Nkota woke up, took his gun and sack, and headed towards Atonga's house just as he had done the other day. He knocked on the door but to his surprise, the always-waiting Atonga was not around.

"That's weird," he muttered to himself.

"Well, maybe he has already gone for some perfectly understandable reason, but what could it be?" Nkota wondered.

He put his sack on his shoulder and walked to the forest. As he got to the first trap, he realised that someone had just removed the prey. He quickly cocked his gun ready to send the heartless thief to an early grave. He moved on to the next trap and, surprisingly, the thief had emptied that one also. He began to quiver.

"This has never happened before. Who would have followed us to the forest that day?" he wondered. He composed himself and headed towards another one. Reaching the trap, he saw someone on their knees trying hard to remove the animal caught in it. He tried not to let the thief know he was there. Just as he was about to pull the trigger, Atonga got up, facing him directly. Years of practice and self-discipline with his custom-made gun enabled him to stop himself committing the worst atrocity in the history of the village.

"What? Atonga? What are you doing here and why are you alone?"

Nkota, furious at the betrayal, aimed the gun at his best friend, but memories of the past were too strong to allow him to breach one of the fundamental laws of nature. He stepped back as Atonga begged for mercy.

For days, Nkota sat in front of his house, waiting patiently to see if he would ever meet with his best friend again. He would go to Atonga's house several times a day but he was never there. The shame and embarrassment was too much for Atonga. Since then, Nkota, not having any friends in the village, would sit in front of his hut alone as he watched people go by. He needed a new friend but where would he find one, and how? He resorted to the bottle.

Every evening he would go to the local beer parlour and drink his sorrows and loneliness away.

One day, when he was returning home from the beer parlour, he realised that someone was following him. Ordinarily he would have reached for his gun, but as this was not a hunting trip, he did not have it with him. He increased the frequency of his steps to flee from the mysterious stranger, but in his stupor he could not walk any faster. Luckily, he got home and banged his door behind him.

The next morning he woke to find a big surprise. A big white dog was standing at the end of Nkota's bed, wagging its tail and leaning forward for affection. The offer was so sincere he could not resist. Nkota knelt down on one knee, picked up the dog's paws and stroked his fur.

"Welcome home, friend," he said.

Since that day, they developed a strong bond, hunting and playing in front of the hut. Nkota would sometimes talk to the dog, wishing he understood him so that they could reminiscence about life. Anytime they went hunting and some of their 'kill' fled, the dog would chase it and bring it back to him. They were a perfect pair for the game. Each morning, the dog would greet him with the same look. He never showed tiredness, resentment, anger or any sign of jealousy.

One day, having come home from hunting, he realised that the dog was behaving strangely. He would spin around and throw up incessantly. He could tell the dog had eaten something poisonous in the forest. Nkota immediately prepared some local herbs for him, but there was nothing he could do to help the animal. A life of loneliness began once again, but this time he had one wish and would do anything to make that wish come true.

The celebration had just begun. Almost everyone in the village marched in procession towards the chief's palace. This time, it was for the inauguration of a would-be hero and the future richest man of the village. In the village, there was an ancient path to riches: if a man can travel to the forbidden forest to fetch a pot of the leaves of a particular tree, he will get everything he desires in life. The gathering at the palace was to offer prayers for the brave hero who was preparing to venture into the unknown.

Nkota - the would-be hero - set off into the forest. A few minutes into the dense woodland, he found himself in the middle of a fierce pride of lions. The look in their eyes betrayed their intentions; to make him a feast. He quickly picked up his already cocked gun, his hands steady on the trigger. The angry and hungry lions did not seem terrified by his act of defence but kept roaring and gnashing their teeth as they moved closer to him. He turned around and around with the gun, pointing it at each lion in turn. After several turnings, he realised that his best possible shot would only kill one of them. Then as if fate had seen his predicament, a big buffalo came running behind the furious predators. He sighed with relief, knowing the beast would divert the blood lust of the angry lions, but, to his surprise, they seemed not to be bothered by the buffalo and kept advancing towards him. Still shaking, terrified and partially blinded by tears, he took a perfect shot, hitting the buffalo in the neck. The buffalo fell down instantly with a loud thud, attracting the attention of the predators. Within a few minutes, a pile of bones was all that remained of the buffalo. He picked up his sack and ran as fast as he could, fleeing from the predators. He kept running through the thick, quiet forest.

Halfway through the journey he came across a long, still river, which he had to cross to get to the other side. He smiled, strapped his gun on his shoulder, and rolled up the bottoms of his trousers, ready to walk through the river. As soon as he stepped into the river, the water started raging, threatening to sweep him away. He managed to get himself back onto the riverbank. The river's turbulence quickly subsided just as he stepped out of it. He became confused, but was not willing to return back empty-handed. He stepped again into the still river, but the river began raging with turbulence once again. Again, he managed to swim back to the riverbank. The river became still again. He stood there for a few minutes. Realising that the silent river raged at him anytime he made an effort, he knelt down by the bank of the river saying, "I have forgiven Atonga. I have nothing against him and I still love him as a brother." The still river began raging fiercely. He was shocked by the new change, but he was sure of himself this time. He put one foot into the fast current and instantly the river became still. He smiled and walked through the river to the other side. He kept on walking, happily whistling, proud of his achievements so far.

After walking for about half a mile, he came across a dark narrow cave full of big bats. The only way he could continue his journey was to go through the cave. As a hunter, he realised that the kind of bats he was seeing in the cave were not ferocious unless they were threatened. He put his gun in his sack and tried to crawl quietly on his knees through the cave. The creatures swarmed, biting into his skin and whipping him with their wings. In throwing his hands around in the air, he hit the biggest of them - which he suspected to be the king of them - and it took tumbles to the ground. Nkota had broken its wing and it lay squeaking in pain. It was as if the others had taken strength from its squeak, enraging them to beat him as hard as they could. Nkota crawled towards the injured one on the ground, picked it up and carefully tied up its broken wing with threads from his sack. The furious creatures stopped beating him with their wings and flew up to the roof of the cave silent and calm. Relieved, he crawled his way through to the exit of the cave.

Nkota kept on walking, whistling and smiling, until he finally made it to the mystery tree. He was stretching out his hands to pluck the leaves when, out of the corner of his eye, he saw a big antelope running towards him. Within a few seconds, the sound of his gun echoed through the thick forest. Oh, how he loved his 'kill'! Unfortunately, this time he had only injured the antelope and it fled. He heard the loud howling of a big fox drawing closer and closer to him. He hid behind the tree, but the fox came towards him with the wounded animal in its mouth. He put the antelope about seven feet in front of Nkota, looked at him with the same gaze as his dog used to do in the morning and ran away. He stood there puzzled, but managed to compose himself and picked up his kill. He left the forest without collecting the leaves from the tree.

The gathered crowd began dancing and singing as their new hero emerged from the forest. The young women were wearing their most special clothing, hoping to be the one to win his affection.

Nkota marched into the palace for an official declaration of success by the king. The king asked him to present to him the mystery leaves. Nkota shook his head, cleared his throat, opened his sack and produced the antelope. The gathered crowd gasped collectively. The king turned away and declared Nkota a failure and a coward. He dismissed him from his presence.

Nkota left the palace smiling with contentment. All he had wished for when he had lost his dear dog was to find out why dogs are one of man's best friends. He'd been asking himself if it was by virtue of the food and warmth with which man provided them or by virtue of natural impulses. The fox had provided the answer. What did he need the mystery leaves for now? At last, his wish had been granted.

The secret strategy for any experiment is to try.

YOU NEVER KNOW

The crowd cheered as the four contestants walked onto the platform. The Campton Contest was the first of its kind, organised to attract many people to the community of Manhattan, Montana. 'A carnival in the making', some would say. Men would be tried, tested and given the opportunity to prove themselves.

"Ladies and gentlemen. Welcome to the first annual Campton Contest," said a voice through a microphone. "We are here today to witness brains and brawn in action. I am Cabby Glover, the manager of today's contest. Before the contestants begin crossing the river, I would like each and every one of you to rise up from your seats and shout as loud as you can to spur them on. Let's welcome the first contestant, Mr. Garby, to the start of the course."

Garby, his braided hair flapping behind his neck, jumped up, waving his hands to the crowds to show his appreciation for their cheers. He stretched out his legs and hands as he gripped the rope. He started slowly and cautiously as the crowd watched in awe. He reached the first obstacle; an open space with two tiny ropes in the middle. Garby was supposed to walk over with a foot on each of the ropes. As he stepped on the rope, he was catapulted sideways but managed to grab the rope by wrapping his legs around it. The crowd gasped, some of them covered their eyes, others their mouths. Others screamed with fear.

"Hold on, people, he will be fine. What he has done is fine, there is only one rule: finishing the course. It doesn't matter how the participants achieve that," said the voice through the microphone. He redirected the crowd's attention to Garby as he prepared himself for the next obstacle.

Garby maintained his grip as he got to the second obstacle. He was supposed to jump over an open space to the other end of the bridge without support with his hands. He stood there for a few seconds before he took the big leap. His right leg landed on the wooden board but his left leg was hanging over the bridge. The crowd rose in fear once again. He tried to get his whole body back on the bridge but he was too heavy. As he tried to get his whole body on the board, he slipped and almost fell into the raging river below. He looked down and began panicking.

"Go on, Garby. You can do it. Go on," the crowd cheered him on. He managed to get back onto the board and headed towards the next challenge. When he got there, he found a single rope, along which he had to swing. Garby gripped with his two hands as he swung his body along. The rope had been designed in such a way that the longer you stay on it, the stronger it would throw your weight around. Because he was slow, the rope began throwing him around. He kept on swinging but unfortunately he lost the 'perfect rhythm' of his body and the rope, and fell into the river. The river's strong current carried him away as he kept on screaming. The crowd started screaming: "Somebody help him, somebody help him." Mr. Cabby kept on laughing uncontrollably through the microphone. He ignored the plight of the first contestant and called the second, Parby, to the start.

Parby was shocked and panicking, but said to himself, "No, I came here to prove my worth and that is what I will do."

Parby began the first obstacle. He started with such speed and determination. He put his two feet on the two tiny ropes. His pace allowed him to maintain a perfect balance and he overcame the obstacle with ease. The crowd stood up to cheer him on and give him their support.

"Good one, good one," Mr. Cabby commended him. Full with pride, he continued as fast as he could to the next obstacle. When he got to the open space, his level of speed once again supported him. He made a big leap and landed in the centre of the board. The crowd went wild. He moved on hastily to the next obstacle.

When he got closer, he realised that at his current pace he would swing a lot on the single rope, which would make him lose his grip, so he clenched onto the rope with both legs and hands. As he kept on pulling his big muscular body along, he started to panic and struggled to keep in time with the movement of the rope. The crowd could see the outlines of his muscles bulge, but he seemed to get strength from their cheering. Everyone began clapping and he managed to go through at that fast pace. Then he got to the last obstacle. The crowd were impressed with his masterful display. He put his right leg on the rolling log and tried running along it at a fast pace. Just as he got to the middle of the log, the high speed caused him to slip. He hopelessly tried to cling on to the log but it was too slippery. He fell into the river as the cheering changed to boos of disappointment.

"Ladies and gentlemen, I guess our 'almost' hero wanted to take a swim." Mr. Cabby laughed. "Well, the first two contestants didn't have what it takes, but let us now welcome our third contestant, Tardy."

Tardy, diminutive, short and slender, stood at the beginning of the course completely confused. The crowd could see his confusion and longed to know what he was going to do.

He started the first obstacle as fast as the second contestant had. Amazingly, his pace allowed him to synchronise his balance with the two tiny ropes and he easily went over the obstacle. At the second obstacle, he was sure of what he wanted to do. *Maybe what I need is a combination of both tactics*, he thought. He slowed his pace and tried to jump on to the board. Just as he jumped, he slipped and found himself hanging on for dear life. His pace was too slow to allow him to get onto the board. He tried to get on the board but he fell into the river. The crowd could not hide their disappointment. He was swept away by the high river current.

"I guess we have another failure! Well, ladies and gentlemen, all is not lost. We have one last contestant hoping to impress us with an astounding performance. Please welcome… Narby."

Narby, tall, heavily-built and muscular, stood at the start with a curious look on his face. "What do I do now? How can this be possible?" He kept asking himself these questions as the crowd cheered incessantly. He leaned forward, ready to face the first obstacle. The cheering grew louder. "Go! Go! Go!" He sniffed in fear and turned away. The crowd began abusing him when he left the platform. But he heard something that challenged his ego.

"I must prove myself," he said. He turned back onto the platform to start the course but Mr. Cabby had already instructed the guards to close it. To his amazement, he saw the other contestants at the other end, fit and dry. The crowd were clapping, shouting and cheering for them. He became confused and went straight to Mr. Cabby's office to request another chance.

A dapper old man sat in an old chair with a cigar in his hand. "Welcome, loser, how can I help you?" he teased. Furious, Narby grabbed the old man's tie, and was ready to strangle him if he was not given the opportunity to have another attempt. The old man seemed unconcerned about his current predicament and he took a puff at his cigar. He kept on laughing uncontrollably at the enraged young man.

"Please sir, relinquish me from your grip and I'll see what I can do." His persuasive tone worked like a charm on the young man, as he let the man go.

"Sit down, young man and let's talk," he said. "I would be more than happy to let you have another go, but I can't. That's not how it works."

Narby was ready to pounce on him again, but this time his opponent defended himself.

"Listen, young man, it doesn't always work this way. 'Had I known…' is what we normally say when we discover our shortcomings. Nevertheless, if we had known what we did not know, it might still not have had any impact on our behaviour. For each day, we hardly walk on paths unfamiliar to us. Life is not a game where our strategies are based on our opponents. It is true that we learn from our experiences, but if we forget yesterday then what have we learned from our experiences? What worked for us today might not work tomorrow. If we can be perfect today, then why should we live for tomorrow? Life is just an experiment. Until we try, we will hardly know, and until we know, we will hardly understand."

Narby rose to his feet, nodding at Mr. Glover's words. He extended his hand to him. "Thank you, Cabby. I guess I will have to take my chances next time!" He smiled and walked away.

Better to die by the sword of love than to live at the mercy of hate.

A MOTHER'S LOVE

Jennifer woke up one night with such fear and paranoia. Kelvin, who was half asleep leapt and pulled her into his arms. "Darling, what's the matter? Did you have a nightmare? Are you alright?" He kept on with the questions so incessantly that she couldn't figure out which one to answer first. She nodded affirmatively to them all as her head rested on his chest. He realised she needed that more than his desire to know what had just happened. She sobbed for about ten minutes, blowing her nose on the hem of her nightgown. He waited patiently for her to compose herself.

She smiled a little, shook her head as she threw her hands in the air, and turned to Kelvin.

"We really were a happy family," she said. "My father would sit down with me and my sisters all night, telling us jokes about how he met our mother. He seemed to remember every detail. He could tell it repeatedly with the same tempo and emotions. God, he was really in love with her. For my mother, he was her whole world. Sometimes, when he stayed late at the office because his work demanded it, she would tell us that he loved us but that he had to work to support us. She would sit up all night waiting for him. When he got back they would have coffee together and laugh all night, as if there was no tomorrow.

"And, sometimes when my mother was late from work because

there was an emergency at the hospital, he would make sure us children had our dinner, put us to bed and sat in the living room waiting for her so that they could have dinner together. It was perfect. We always had the assurance of their smiles and togetherness. Every Christmas we would go for a family ice skating trip to Colmar. My younger sister loved skating, so we would watch her spin around on the ice with my father. We always wanted to stay close. We would book a family suite where all of us would be together, talking all night until we dozed off.

"It all started to change when my father came home drunk one night. My mother had been sitting up waiting for him to return or even just call, but no, this time there was a distance between them. As my mother tried to help him get his shirt off, she found a trace of lipstick on his collar. She didn't want to jump to conclusions, so she asked him politely what it was and where he got it.

"It was as if something had possessed my father - he turned and slapped my mother. She stood there, shocked. My father had never laid a hand on her before. She tried not to cry aloud so we would not hear her. But I was awake that time and I could hear my mother sobbing. I rushed to their room screaming. My mother quickly came out to meet me; she probably did not want me to see my father in that state.

"Since then, my father began staying out late. Sometimes he would not come home at all. My mother was afraid he might hit her in front of us, so she never bothered to ask him where he had been. He grew very distant from us. We sometimes forgot that we had a father. Anytime we asked my mother, she would say, 'No, honey, Dad is just having a hard time at the office. It's just temporary and everything will go back to the way it was.' But I could tell something was wrong.

"With time, he refused to provide money for the upkeep of the house. Since my mother was now handling all the domestic chores alone - my two sisters and I were too young to help her out - she was forced to get a part-time job at the hospital: it was the only way she could make sure we were not neglected. After a few months with us at home, she realised that we needed money if we were to survive. She had to take another job at a local dry cleaner's. I could feel her pain and suffering each time she came home to prepare dinner for us. I wanted to do something to help, but I was too young to do much.

"We were managing without a father and a husband, but still were blessed enough to have our normal ceremonial birthdays and parties.

"Just as we thought things could not get worse, our worst fear knocked on our front door. My mother was out at work when my father came home with this mean and bitter woman who stared at us as if our very presence revolted her."

Kelvin realised she wanted to cry again. He took her hand in his and gently pressed it.

"I mean in our own parents' house!" she continued. "We never realised the nightmare was only just beginning. My father felt no shame in keeping her in the house even when my mother was around. My mother was no longer sleeping in their marital bedroom. That merciless man had kicked her out and was always shamelessly shouting and screaming with that woman in the bedroom. My mother would cry every night after we had slept.

"After my mother had left for work in the morning, we became slaves for his mistress. Could you imagine bossing ten-year-old children around like they were twenty-year-old house maids?"

Jennifer shook her head in dismay. Kelvin could sense the fury and frustrations in her voice. He knew he had to keep quiet to allow her to release her anger. She sniffled and turned her face away.

"I remember one day my little sister accidentally spilt milk on the kitchen floor and that woman came screaming at her. She pulled her ear so hard that it began to bleed. My father watched without saying a word."

Jennifer burst into tears, as she could not take it any longer. Kelvin pulled her into his arms once again. "It's okay, it's okay. It's over. It's past. I am here for you and I love you. I would give up everything for you and our children." He took her head in his hands and looked deeply into her eyes. "I promise to be there for you to the end."

She could tell she needed him desperately. She embraced him tightly, still sobbing. She started kissing him as they passionately enjoyed each other's bodies.

The children were waiting patiently by the car. It was time for them to go on their usual family fishing trip. The children loved to watch their parent's fish as they taught them a few lessons about it. She would tell them that 'fishing teaches people one big lesson about life: as you wait for the fish to come to the bait, you do not know when and what kind of fish you will get. But patiently, you wait in optimism. That's how life works; whatever you seek in life, you have to be patiently optimistic.'

They would grill their catch by the river and enjoy the flavour of ginger and garlic. It always brought them together.

Kelvin came out of the house in a suit, his luggage in his hand. "Honey, have you forgotten?" she asked. "We have to go fishing with the kids."

"Oh, yeah." He leaned back defensively. "Sorry, honey, I forgot to tell you. I have this important meeting at the office with some new investors." Kelvin had never before given Jennifer any reason to doubt his word. The children moaned with disappointment as they walked away. "Hey, hey, guys. Come on, it's only temporary. I will go with you next time."

He slammed his car door and drove off.

"Mummy, does it mean we are not going anymore?" She could tell what the children were thinking. Or could she? She tried to force a smile to make them happy. "No, we are. You know what, just get the bags in the car and we will leave now. Daddy will come later when he is done with his work."

She could not lie to herself about the sudden change. He had never missed any of their fishing trips before. When the children had gone back into the house to get their bags, she called his secretary to verify his excuse.

For a minute, the clock stopped and she froze. "What? No. Not Kelvin, surely." She reasoned with herself that at least she had found out; but she wished it didn't have to be in this way and at this time. By the time the children came back with their bags she was standing there speechless. *No. I have to be strong for them,* she thought. She wiped away the tiny teardrops that had built in her eyes.

"Come on, get in. It's time to go," she said to them. She tried not to contemplate the awful news so that she could give the children the fun they had been anticipating.

They sat in the boat on the River Brue as she held on to the fishing rod. They began chatting happily, while the children ate their lunch. It had taken longer than usual to get their grilled fish and garlic. One of the children managed to splash sauce all over her shirt, so Jennifer leaned into the river to scoop up some water with which to clean it off. She slipped, lost her balance and fell into the river. Beneath the surface of the murky water, she wished she had not skipped her swimming lessons. She could not swim and the children were too young to save her.

She stared at their weeping faces as she tried helplessly to swim over. Her worst nightmares were being realised.

Who will love my children? She thought. Kelvin had promised to love them all forever, but now even he could not be trusted. *What will happen if he brings her into the house permanently? Even if he keeps his promise, will he live long enough to comfort them?*

She could not bear the thought that her whispers of comfort would be unheard, or that her children would not feel the warm embrace of her open arms after she was gone. Finally, she came to a decision. She reached for the edge of the boat and tipped it over, drowning the children with her.

Boats and all of the divers in the Somerset community searched every inch of the river in the biggest search of its kind. A mother and her three children had disappeared without a trace. Impossible! One of the divers discovered their bodies under the water and motioned for everyone to help bring them up. What emerged was a mystery that the community has not been able to unravel ever since: the mother had wrapped her arms around all three children and they had all died together. At the inquest everyone had gasped.

"Was it intentional or an accident?" They all asked.

A woman ran as fast as she could to the bodies and screamed, "She is an evil woman. She killed her children out of spite after her husband cheated on her!" Most of the townspeople turned to look at her. Kelvin's promiscuity was a shock to them. Inevitably, it would be a topic of conversation at their future gatherings.

"Well, every man has the right to debate life's mysteries, but only few are privileged to understand them," said Mickey, the leader of the search team, shaking his head.

Kelvin stood there dumbfounded, but his efforts to shed a tear proved futile. This shocking and tragic event took him straight back to his childhood. The memories he had tried all his life to erase now came alive. He could see it in his mind's eye.

His mother had left him when he was young, without giving any reason. He could remember his father violently arguing with his mother the night she packed her suitcase, but he was too young to understand why. His father had never mentioned his absent wife since. Kelvin had grown up without a mother's love. One day, when he was a little older, he found a letter in his father's book stash. He was curious so he opened the letter. He could barely make out his mother's handwriting, but he tried his best to read what was written.

"Dear Kelvin,

I know you will never forgive me when you find out that I abandoned you. I do not intend to justify my actions, but I am sorry. It was for your own good that I left. Please try to remember that there is nothing I long for more than to have you in my arms again. Mum."

Tears had rolled down Kelvin's face as he turned the letter over and he wrote,

"Dear Mummy,

I may not remember you too well, but I miss your smiles that made Daddy come home early every day to help me with my homework. I miss your pastries that made Daddy stay all night with you in the bedroom. I

miss your arms that always gave me hope for tomorrow. I miss your lovely voice that always put me to sleep every night. Above all, I miss your duties in the house because my new mummy makes me do all the work and I cannot go out to play with my friends. Wherever you are, I still wait for your promise."

The thoughts that always incited pain and anger now nourished his agony. It now became meaningful. He walked towards the bodies and pulled the sheet up to cover their faces, saying, "I envy you, my children. In birth, you came through her, and in death, you left through her. Farewell to a love well displayed."

He wiped his eyes with the back of his left hand and walked away, his heart fraught with guilt and regret.

ACKNOWLEDGEMENTS

I am very grateful to George, Ben, Cecilia, Jane, Graham, Clare and Justice for their immense support and belief in me throughout the challenge involved in writing this book.

To Tom, I say a big thank you. You are a true friend.